W9-AMB-893

DEADLY PERCEPTION

By Vicki Long

This book is a work of fiction. People, places, events, and situations in this story are purely fictional. Any resemblance to actual persons, living or dead, is coincidental.

© 2004 by Vicki Long. All rights reserved.

No part of this book may be reproduced, stored in a retrieval system, or transmitted by any means, electronic, mechanical, photocopying, recording, or otherwise, without written permission from the author.

ISBN: 1-4140-3802-X (ebook)
ISBN: 1-4140-3803-8 (Paperback)

This book is printed on acid free paper.

1st Books - rev. 12/11/03

To see other books by Vicki Long, go to 1stBooks.com
The Destiny Family

Deadly Perception

Once Tim noticed his uncle standing by the door, all conversation stopped. Janet was not amused. "Don't you know how to knock?" The spell was broken; they wouldn't get any more done so she closed her drawing pad and prepared to leave.

Sam realized his mistake. Tim was staring out the window, not sure how much his uncle had heard. Janet touched her patient's arm, before leaving the room without saying a word to Sam.

He followed her out of the room grabbing her arm. "You don't have to leave."

"We're done for the day." Janet said, giving him an icy look until he released her arm.

"I'm family. My being there shouldn't bother you or Tim."

"You are still a police detective."

"That's my job."

"Next time, wait outside so I can do my job."

Sam watched her walk briskly down the hall towards the elevator. He should be sorry he upset her, but all he could do was smile. She was gorgeous when she was mad. Her eyes flashed fire. Sam wondered if that was the only time her eyes caught that spark. Their paths did not cross again for several months.

Thanks to my family for their encouragement and support.
Thanks to Jennifer for assistance with editing.

To those that dream of writing, put pen to paper
and let the words flow.

x

Chapter One

"Do you want me to pose for you?" Sadie asked. She patted her tangled dirty hair as if she had just returned from the beauty salon.

"No, Sadie. You know I like to draw from real life." Janet Leigh handed Sadie what was left of her bag lunch. Sadie lost interest in posing for her and explored the contents of the bag.

"You eat like a bird. Look at all the food you have left." Sadie mumbled in Janet's general direction. She carefully pulled off the crust of the sandwich she was eating, and threw tiny pieces to the waiting pigeons. Even if Sadie had only one piece of bread and no promise of another meal, she would share it with her feathered friends.

Most days at lunchtime, you could find Janet in the park drawing pictures of her friends and fellow picnickers. Her lunch was packed with great care each day knowing that she would give most of it away.

It was such a beautiful spring day; the sun was warm, but the air was still cool. After a bleak winter, the bright day brought many to the park at midday. Riverside Park is a long narrow Park stretching from 72nd street Northward along the Hudson River, in the upper west side of Manhattan. Built on several levels, the park allows visitors to walk through trees and gardens, up and down stairs, through tunnels, around monuments, and along the Hudson River. There are areas for the athletically inclined and areas for those that simply want to doze in the park's splendor.

Janet sat on a bench beneath a blossom-covered tree with drawing pad and pencil sketching the elderly lady sitting on the next bench. As her pencil glides across the parchment, the chiseled features and deep lines of the woman's face are captured in a drawing so very lifelike. In realistic detail she draws what she sees, the unique qualities that make Sadie special.

Janet has a gift, a most unusual gift. As she sketches the people she watches, she sees more than just the outward characteristics of her models. Studying each individual as she draws them, bits and pieces about the individuals come to mind. She likes to think of it as a sixth sense, almost like she catches a glimpse of that person's inner soul.

As she finishes her sketch, she signs and dates it. In a corner she puts Sadie's name and writes a sentence or two about her. The words flow through her pencil to the paper as if by magic. Her sixth sense has a mind of its own. It is nothing she has ever been able to control.

Janet closed her drawing pad. "See you Sadie! It's time

to go back to work."

"Bye, Dearie! Take Care!" Sadie carefully folded the lunch bag and put it into her pocket. She smiled at Janet as she waved.

On her way out of the park she passed another friend. "How's your cold, Gladys?"

"Getting better." She sniffed and smiled up at Janet from her bench.

Janet reached over and gave the woman's shoulder a gentle squeeze. From her purse, she pulled out a package of tissues, which brought another sniff and a smile from Gladys. "Take care of yourself."

With a wave, she continued on the short walk back to her office. Sadie, Gladys, and others watched Janet as she walked away. Stylishly dressed in her own unique way, Janet's tall slender figure often caught admiring glances as she walked to and from her office each day. Her short wavy brown hair frames her face where bright blue eyes search the world around her for the interesting and the unusual.

Janet had been working in the city about five years. It was the bright spring sunshine that drew her out of her office that first day. She found it very relaxing to sit in the fresh air, to meet and make new friends while she drew pictures of the people and scenery around her.

Unless the weather was really nasty she went to the park to eat lunch. On the really bad days in winter, she often went to the park to bring blankets to any poor souls who braved the elements instead of fleeing to the shelters. The thought of any of them spending a night on the streets made her so sad.

The more homeless people she met, the more she wanted to help them. In the lunch she packed each day, she often put more than food: moist towelettes, a toothbrush, toothpaste, or a comb. These subtle gestures of friendship were accepted good-naturedly as if she always packed them in her lunch.

Of course, she met a lot of people in the park who weren't homeless: nannies with prams and toddlers, tourists visiting New York City, families visiting the area picnicking, business men and women like herself who were enjoying the fresh air and sunshine, and others who were just passing through. There were also the down and out that often spent many hours in the park, not knowing where else to go or just not inclined to do much at all.

Strolling until she saw a free bench or space to sit, Janet would nibble at her lunch watching people. A certain person or scene would capture her interest and then she would pick up her drawing pad and pencil. Her lunch was soon forgotten.

Her favorite drawing was of a young couple sharing their deli lunch on the grass. Flowers bloomed close by. Green trees surrounded the area. Their animated conversation was too far away to hear, but they were close enough for Janet to see the love they shared. The girl's straw hat, meant to shield her from the sun, framed her smiling face. Her equally handsome mate was so enthralled by their conversation that he noticed no one else.

It reminded Janet that it was possible to find that one person who was your soul mate. This was one of the few drawings that she finished in pastels and later framed. Out of the hundreds of drawings she'd done, only a few had touched her in this way. It now hangs in her office where she can see it everyday.

Chapter Two

Sketching interesting people has been a past time of Janet's since childhood. Even when she was young, her drawing took in every detail and showed a gifted talent. Her father did not encourage her gift. He was adamant that his motherless child had to learn a marketable trade that would allow her to take care of herself. The world was cruel, but she would be ready.

Her sketches and the people in them became her friends. When she sketched she was never lonely. It was not enough to just draw her friends; she had to know their names. So her gift became a way to meet people, to get out and talk to people. Rarely did she give the drawings away. On those occasions she would usually sign her name in an inconspicuous place, sometimes within the drawing itself rather than standing alone at the bottom of the page.

Janet preferred drawing the eyes first. But, because her subjects usually didn't sit still and pose for her, she started with the background. When her subjects realized she was drawing them, they would glance over to watch her. Then she could see their eyes, their facial expressions, and the way the light played on their features.

As her pencil flies across the page it captures her model in such a realistic fashion. Janet is able to show the sparkles of laughter and the fine lines that illustrate the true character of that person. In a week, she could fill a drawing pad. Most evenings, she takes a few minutes to look at her drawings, maybe filling in a few more details before moving on to the next drawing. Her subjects remain familiar to her once she has drawn them.

She has files full of drawings. Janet likes to file them by name or location. If she met one person often, it was common for her to have a dozen drawings of that individual. At the end of each year, she packed some of them away in boxes. Her drawings were so real to her that she had never thrown one away.

As one may have already guessed, Janet does not make her living by sketching her friends. Since art was important to her, her career had to include some aspect of art. Managing an art gallery sounded like great fun when she was in college, but wasn't practical. She thought about fashion design, but not many agreed with her idea of fashion.

Some aspect of business seemed like a good choice. A friend in college talked her into taking an advertising class with her. A class project caught the interest of her professor, and he encouraged her to major in advertising. With his help she was able to get a summer job at a small agency. By fall she had grown tired of drawing imaginary ideas. She preferred to draw from real life, but she had to make a living doing something so she stuck with it.

There was more to her gift than talent. Her drawing pad went wherever she went, pencils always sharpened and ready. When she got one of these feelings it was as if she was obsessed. Her pad was open with pencil in hand before she even knew what was happening. Stopping in her tracks she would turn to the direction of the strongest vibrations, and open her mind. Sometimes it wasn't a person she drew, but a place. She would see a place, and then after she started to draw she would see the people who would pass that way. Seldom had she waited around to see if the images she drew actually happened as she saw them. Mostly they were good things that she saw, and it just didn't seem right to witness what happened in other people's lives. It felt like she was spying.

For her own benefit she got in the habit of putting the date and time on each drawing. On the back or in the corner, she would write the story line or a few sentences about the person or place.

This was a talent and a curse. On occasion she would be in the middle of a conversation with her associates, and they would start talking about the very thing she had seen in one of her visions. Without thinking she would fill in details that no one else knew. She was so sure of the details that they would ask if she had been there when it happened. Embarrassed, her favorite line became "No, my friend is a reporter at the newspaper." This line usually worked, but she had to come up with a name. She actually did know one of the newspaper reporters from college, Stewart Mackenzie, but they rarely talked. Fortunately, no one else knew him or bothered to check out her story.

She didn't think they could handle the truth without thinking she was crazy. How many people did you run into on a daily basis that were clairvoyant? Not many. At least she had never met anyone else with the same gift.

Not many knew her secret. She had tried to explain it to her father once, but the look on his face had stopped her. Her father just thought she had an overactive imagination. Not once did he take what she said seriously.

It became very lonely having no one to share her secret with. She had friends at work, but no one who got close enough to see the truth. Her friends just saw her as a talented artist, a creative associate that was an asset to their team. Occasionally, she was asked out to dinner, a movie, or to a party. Her first impression of the people she dated often made her wary of getting close to them. She could sense things about them that they would never share with others. If she let them get close enough to witness one of her visions, they no longer wanted to be associated with her.

On one particular date, she had sketched the handsome man sitting across from her. When the drawing was complete, she had drawn in a high building in the background with flames coming out of a high window where a young boy stood. The flames were all around him. A woman holding the hand of another small boy was running from the building.

Her date insisted she show him the drawing. She hesitated, knowing there would be no other dates with him once he saw it. The truth in her drawings had scared many others away. Resigning herself to expect the worst, she let him see the drawing.

"This is very good." He said as he looked at the portrait dominating most of the page, but when he saw the scene in the background, his face grew pale. "How did you know? Who told you?" He asked angrily.

"I felt your sadness, your grief." She gave him a tentative smile. "It wasn't your fault. You know that."

"No, it was my fault. It should have been me that died in that fire. It's was all my fault. I was trying to light a cigarette that I stole from my mother's purse." He ran his hand through his hair as he told the story. "I sat there smoking in the bedroom. My little brother ran in and stole the matches, and ran to his room. I forgot about it and an hour or so later I woke up smelling smoke. Mom's room was closer so I woke her up first, but we couldn't get near Nick's room. The flames were too hot. The firemen tried to reach him by

10

ladder, but it was too late. We saw him at the window one moment, and then he was gone."

"You didn't start that fire. It's not your fault." She offered gently.

"I should have gone after him and taken the matches away. I remember telling him not to play with the matches. He was only five, and very curious about everything. I should have taken them away. I shouldn't have been smoking."

"I'm sorry, if I upset you." She noticed that he hadn't touched his food.

"Let's go. I'm not hungry." She followed him out of the restaurant. They drove back to her apartment in silence.

She thanked him and opened the car door to leave. At the last minute he stopped her. "Do you ever give your drawings away?"

Opening her drawing pad, she carefully tore it out of her pad, and handed it to him.

"Thank you. I'll call you." As soon as she shut the door, he sped away.

He actually did call her the next day. "I just wanted to thank you for the drawing, and for being there. I've never told anyone about that before."

"Would you like to come over for supper tomorrow night?" She offered, thinking he was still interested.

"No, I don't think so." He said immediately, and then realized how harsh he sounded. "You're very pretty, but I'd just be too uncomfortable."

"It's O.K. I understand." She told him good-bye, and hung up.

She hadn't dated much since then. That was the day she decided to go back to college and study Psychiatry. The many years of hard studying it took to become a doctor were worth it for her to be able to use her gift to help others. Her drawings became part of her note taking. She was able to sense her patient's inner fears, their grief, or the history that was at the core of all their problems. Rarely did anyone see these drawings. They were private, containing the inner secrets of her patients.

Except for her forays into the park each day, her work was her life. The only social life she had were the banquets, parties and receptions she went to for the many charities she contributed to. Occasionally, another doctor would invite her to dinner or the theatre, but if she needed a date for a function she often took her young assistant, Les. He was gay, and loved to dress up for a night out on the city. When she didn't want the hassle of searching for the appropriate escort, Les was a fun date. He was also her best friend. They took care of each other when they got sick, had keys to each other's apartments, and even borrowed each other's clothes on occasion.

Les' passion was the stage. He had auditioned for just about every show on or off Broadway since he moved to

New York. Finally, he found his way into her office as a temporary and they just clicked. Les had been her assistant for four years. He still worked in the theatre, but now he directed plays for children in the area schools in the evenings and on weekends.

Janet did not discuss her sixth sense with Les. Her gift was something she didn't understand herself. How could anyone else understand? She was content with her life the way it was, lonely at times, but content.

Chapter Three

Because her drawing pad went wherever she went, Janet drew comfort knowing she had it with her. If she had one of her visions, she didn't need to draw what she saw, but she just found it easier to illustrate these visions. Drawing helped to pull all the details together, and the drawing served as a record of the vision for future reference.

At an early age, she had learned not to fight these visions when they came. Any effort to try to block the visions only resulted in a terrible headache. Since back then the visions were usually about pleasant things, she found no reason to fight them. Having one of these visions was like watching a film clip in slow motion.

As she grew older the visions were not always pleasant, but by then she had learned that life wasn't always pleasant. If she had a premonition about something that would happen, she would watch from a distance to see if the vision came true. After a while when she had learned to trust the visions would come true, she didn't always want to watch the vision unfold.

Premonitions for bad things kept coming and she began an inner battle with herself. "Could I have stopped it from happening?" or "Would I really have put myself in danger if I tried to keep it from happening?"

Every morning she read the newspaper to follow the events, sometimes even clipping the articles out to put with her drawings. When someone died during one of these events, she decided to get more involved. Her drawing pad helped. Janet found that she could delay people by offering to draw them, or at least distract them through conversation.

Most of the time, her interference changed the events she had seen in her vision, but other times the events happened anyway. She felt better for at least trying.

After she lived and worked in Manhattan for a while, it became difficult not to get involved. Day to day, and week to week, she saw the same people and couldn't help but take an interest in them. At first she just shared her lunch everyday with one of her homeless friends. Over time she learned what shelters and food kitchens were available, where the clinics were located, and where they could go for drug or alcohol treatment.

Little by little she started to meddle in their lives. For instance, Sadie had a younger sister that was still living in the city. Janet asked questions as she drew her picture. After several weeks she had pieced together enough information to find Elizabeth, Sadie's sister.

She met with Elizabeth alone to prepare her for the desperate appearance of her sister. Janet didn't want her to be too shocked or give Sadie a negative impression that would scare her away. Janet suggested that Elizabeth start having her lunch in the park, and to meet Sadie by chance. After they had shared their lunch several times and everything went well, it would only be polite for Elizabeth to invite Sadie to her home. She warned Elizabeth that Sadie could reject any offers of help. The situation had to be handled in a delicately, leaving Sadie the option of stopping by for a visit. Janet learned how much stubborn pride the homeless have despite their situation.

Janet didn't see Sadie for several days and she was beginning to worry about her. She saw Elizabeth sitting on a bench sitting with another lady. Janet did a double take, and then stopped in front of them with a smile. "Wow! Sadie! You clean up nice!"

Elizabeth grinned at her sister. Sadie's face turned a pretty pink. She had on a skirt and neatly pressed blouse, and her hair was cut in a very becoming way. Touching the collar of her blouse, she smiled up at Janet. "Thank you." The look that passed between them told her the thank you was for more than the compliment.

Smiling at the pretty picture they made sitting there together, Janet offered to draw them. When she finished the drawing, she had tears in her eyes. The only thing she saw as she drew was the two of them living happily together. With a flourish she signed the drawing and handed it to them. Sadie had tears in her own eyes as she looked up at Janet.

She kissed Sadie's cheek and gathered her things to leave. "Got to get back to work. Would you give this to one of our friends for me?" Handing Sadie her lunch bag, she waved and walked away.

Sadie got up and took Janet's lunch to Gladys a few benches away. She touched her forehead to see if she was running a fever. "Gladys, Elizabeth and I are going to the clinic after lunch so Elizabeth can get her allergy shot. How about going with us?" Gladys had been sick off and on for months, and she had resisted all attempts to help her.

Gladys looked Sadie in the eyes to see if she was telling the truth or tricking her. "O.K. if you stay there with me. I don't trust strangers."

Sadie smiled. "Sure. Eat your lunch. Elizabeth and I are going to feed the pigeons."

From that day on Sadie and Elizabeth came to the park to feed the pigeons and to do what they could for their friends old and new. Janet had showed Sadie her life could hold purpose and was full of possibilities. Elizabeth had been lonely too, but now they shared the love of family and found something meaningful they could do together.

Chapter Four

Janet didn't draw just her homeless friends; she drew many people on her forays into the park. One day as she sketched the children playing in the park, her eyes were pulled towards a little boy. As she watched him the ball he was playing with rolled her way. Picking up the ball, she held it out to him as he ran over to her. For a brief moment she looked into his eyes. What she saw there surprised and shocked her.

"Thank you, Lady!" He said as he claimed the ball.

"You're welcome!" She smiled at him with tears glistening on her lashes.

He smiled at her, and then ran back to his friends.

"No," she whispered, "He's such a sweet little boy." She saw pain, and what was going to happen to him. What should she do? Who could she tell? She knew when it would happen and where. There had to be something she could do. There were still a few days left.

Janet moved to a bench closer to where the little boy's nanny sat with another nanny. Flipping to a new page she started sketching the little boy and his friends at play. The nanny glanced over at her from time to time, but decided they had nothing to fear from her. When she finished the sketch, she signed it and gathered her things to leave.

"Hi! I'm Janet." She smiled at them and offered the drawing to the nanny. "Would you like to have it? I hope you don't mind. He's such a cute little boy."

The nanny looked at the drawing and smiled brightly up at Janet. "You're very good. Thank you. I can keep it?"

"It's yours." Janet smiled, and then turned to leave.

"His name is Trevor." She called out to stop her. "Thank you. I'm Therese." She offered her hand.

"Very nice to meet you. Maybe we'll run into each other again. Bye for now." With a wave to little Trevor, Janet slowly walked away.

When she got back to the office, Janet was still visibly upset. Les followed her into her office. "What's wrong?"

"A child is in danger. I need to take two hours for lunch tomorrow and Wednesday. On Thursday, I must have the whole afternoon free."

The concern in her eyes touched Les. "No problem. You'll let me know if I can do anything to help."

Smiling her thanks, Janet touched his cheek. "Was that Mrs. Taylor I saw in the waiting room?" That was her way of saying it was time to get to work.

Walking to the same place in the park the next day, she

sighed with relief when she saw them both there. "Hello! Nice to see you again."

Therese stood and welcomed her. "I was hoping we would see you. Mrs. Calloway, Trevor's mom, she loved your drawing. We are going to frame it and hang it in Trevor's room."

"You're very kind." Janet sat down on the bench next to theirs.

"This is my friend Grace. She and her Daniel meet us here everyday. The boys eat their sandwiches quickly so they can go play." They watched as the boys ran after their ball.

"Pleased to meet you." She smiled and nodded, then watched the boys. "I come to the park everyday and walk around until I find a pleasant place to eat my lunch."

Grace nodded towards her drawing pad. "You are an artist? Where can we go to see your work?"

Janet smiled. "It's just a hobby. I'm a Psychiatrist."

Both nannies looked surprised. The ball came rolling towards them, making further explanation unnecessary. The boys retrieved their ball and ran off again. They talked while they ate their lunches. Janet asked them where they lived and how far it was to the park.

It was the next day before she felt comfortable asking what route they took to and from the park. She told them where her office was located, saying she had hoped they passed that way so she could see them more often. Therese said she usually stopped at the market on their way home to pick up some things for the cook.

Thursday was the day. Janet told Therese that she had the afternoon off. Lingering at the park with them, she hoped to delay their departure. "Maybe I could walk a ways with you? It's such a beautiful day."

"That would be nice." Therese agreed.

Janet smiled down at Trevor. "Do you think we could hold hands?"

Trevor looked up at her shyly, looked at Therese for approval, and then took her hand. Keeping a steady conversation going with little Trevor and Therese, she walked slowly.

About a block from the old Prince theatre, she saw a coffee shop that sold ice cream. Looking at Trevor with delight, she asked, "Let's stop for ice cream.

Therese looked at her watch, then at the excited look on her charge's face. "I must call home so they don't worry."

"Great! What kind do you like? Trevor and I will go stand in line."

Therese reached for her cell phone and stayed just outside the door while she made her call. As she finished her call, she heard a noise and turned just in time to see three people shot in front of the Prince Theatre. The car with the gunmen was speeding its way towards her. Backing towards the doorway, she pulled out a small notebook and wrote down what she could see of the license plate as the car raced away.

Janet was carrying a tray with their ice cream, holding Trevor's hand tightly. Therese's anguished eyes met Janet's over Trevor's head. "We should eat our ice cream before it melts." Janet said, but her eyes said they should protect Trevor from what happened.

Once they sat down, Trevor dug into his ice cream. Therese and Janet took small bites, just making the motions of eating. Therese was shaking. She picked up her notebook and wrote down the color of the car, and then put the pen and paper on the table.

Janet gently picked up the pen and notebook. Printing slowly to try to match Therese's writing style, she filled in the rest of the license plate number and the make of the car. With a shrug, she handed them back to Therese.

"You knew?" Surprise filled her eyes as she realized. "You saved us. How?"

"I can't explain it. I just knew."

A policeman came into the ice cream parlor. Janet reached across the table and squeezed Therese's hand. "Did anyone in here see anything?" he asked.

An older lady sitting nearby spoke up. "What happened?"

"There was a shooting just down the street." He said, looking around the shop at the other people standing at the counter and sitting at tables. "Did anyone see anything?"

Therese got up from the table with her notebook. She didn't want Trevor to hear what she might have to say to the policeman. "I was making a phone call on my cell just outside the door and heard a noise." Therese told him, tearing the page out of her notebook and handing it to him.

"Fantastic!" After getting her name and phone number, he hastily pulled a card from his pocket and thrust it into her hand. "I've got to go." Excited to get such good information, he ran out of the door to the cruiser, jumping in as his partner sped away.

Therese let out a breath and sat back down. As she thought again of what could have happened, she began to cry. Trevor didn't understand why she was crying. "Do you have a booboo?" He offered her a sticky kiss as he crawled on her lap.

"No, I'm O.K, but I could really use a hug." Therese hugged him to her. "I love you, Trevor."

"Luvs you." He said, grinning up at her. Trevor did not waste a minute before turning around and digging into her ice cream.

She started laughing. "Hey!" Trevor giggled, and then fed a spoonful to Therese getting more on her face than in her mouth. They all laughed.

Therese whispered, "Thank you!"

"You are very welcome!"

As they got up to leave, Janet gave Therese one of her business cards. "You can call me anytime. In case you just need to talk." She gave each of them a hug. "Bye. I hope I see you in the park sometime soon." Janet almost skipped back to the office.

Later when Therese talked to the policeman, he told her that they had caught the men. He thanked her for her quick thinking.

"It could have been us that got killed. Our new friend, Janet, talked us into stopping for ice cream." Therese still couldn't stop thinking about it. "She saved us. I think she knew what was going to happen."

"You really think she knew what was going to happen? That's doesn't seem possible unless she knew the killers."

"I'm sure she didn't. Dr. Janet Leigh is a Psychiatrist."

"How long have you known her?"

"Only about four days. She insisted on walking with us today, and then made sure we stopped for ice cream."

"How could she know what was going to happen?" He asked, thinking Therese was in shock.

"She knew." Therese was sure of it.

The officer made a few inquiries about Janet, but found no reason to suspect she had anything to do with the drive by shooting. He finally dropped it, believing that Therese was mistaken.

Chapter Five

"O.K., I admit it. You are one tough guy." Janet shook her head in frustration. "I always had a soft spot for the strong silent type." Pleased that she had coaxed a small smile to his rugged face, she continued to draw in silence.

Instinct told her he needed her in some way. That was the only reason she kept looking for him each day. He was very quiet. After several days she found out his name was Greg. He wouldn't accept her lunch, but always politely said, "No thank you."

Greg resisted her attempts to help him. She knew he slept on the same park bench each night. From drawing him, she learned he collected bottles and cans to get money. Janet had never seen him drink or smelled it on him so she assumed he used the money for food.

Janet tried several times to get closer to Greg so she could help him. One day as she was walking through the park on her way back from a late morning appointment, she saw Greg sitting on his bench eating. Stopping in front of him, she laughed. "Your secret is out. That's why you won't share my lunch with me. You've already eaten by the time I stop by." Janet teased him.

Greg really did like her persistence, he couldn't help but smile. "My secret's out."

His cultured voice surprised Janet. She was pleased to be having a conversation with him, finally.

"Let's start over. I'm Janet Leigh." She held out her hand.

Smiling, Greg shook it. "I'm Greg."

"Would you mind?" She asked, opening her drawing pad.

Greg shrugged, and went back to eating his meal.

Janet sat on the next bench and sketched. He had a very distinguished face. She wished she knew what had happened to him that caused him to live like this. What she saw was frightening. Janet quit drawing. "Since we've become friends, maybe you would like to come home with me tonight, have a home cooked meal, a hot shower, and a real bed for a night?"

Shaking his head, Greg refused. "You are a really sweet lady, but I like my bench."

With deep concern, Janet kept trying. "Please, just for one night? You can't sleep here tonight. You have to sleep somewhere else tonight. How about staying in my office tonight? You can guard it for me." Greg kept shaking his head. "Please, at least find another bench. It's not safe here

26

tonight."

Their eyes met, and he could see that she knew something he didn't. His gut told him to listen to her. "I'll find somewhere else to sleep, but only for one night."

Smiling, Janet gave him her business card and enough money for a phone call. He took both without argument.

Restless after she left, he wandered around all afternoon, collecting cans as he looked for a good place to stay that night. He was turned away at both of the missions that he knew about because they were already full. Looking at the address of Janet's office building, Greg walked until he found it. In the back of the building, he found a fire escape. Climbing up to the second floor, he made his bed on the iron floor using cardboard for a mattress.

Waking early as usual, Greg climbed down and headed slowly back to the park, looking for cans and bottles on the way. On his bench, he found another man half covered with newspaper. "Hey! Hey!" Greg shook the man to wake him and tell him he was trespassing.

The man's hand fell, dangling towards the ground. Upon closer inspection, he could see blood, lots of blood. Panic set in and Greg ran until he found a policeman.

They were waiting for her when she arrived at the office. Les was just pouring them some coffee.

"Good Morning!"

"Dr. Leigh?"

"Yes, what's wrong? Greg is one of my friends." She smiled at him.

Relieved that Janet had arrived, Greg began sipping his coffee.

"Mr. Franklin found a man who had been murdered. The man was sleeping on a bench, the bench where he usually sleeps. Understandably, he was upset to find a dead man on his favorite bench. He gave me your card when I asked if there was anyone we could call." The officer introduced himself as Sgt. George Nelson. "Mr. Franklin needs to come down to the police station to make a statement. Do you have time to go down there with us?"

"Sure! Les?"

"Go, already covered." Les knew she would help anyone she could and he admired her for it. "Wait!" Going into the kitchen, he brought out a muffin that he had brought in for his own breakfast and offered it to Greg.

Greg started to refuse, but after looking at Janet, took the muffin. "Thank you!" He offered his hand to Les, and Les took it without hesitation.

Janet sat with Greg in the back of the police car. She reached across the seat and squeezed his hand for reassurance. When they arrived, Greg Franklin was fascinated by the police station. They were asked to wait a few minutes in a row of chairs on the second floor where desks were scattered throughout a large room. Greg watched the activity around them.

Across the room, Officer Nelson was filling in his Chief and a detective with what he knew. "Who's the lady?" The detective asked.

"Dr. Janet Leigh, a Psychiatrist who works to help the homeless. She's active with a lot of charities. I've seen her name in the newspaper a few times." Officer Nelson admired Janet.

"Not bad looking either. I'll take this one." The detective offered, walking away without waiting for a response.

"Dr. Leigh, Mr. Franklin, I'm Detective Sam Warren. Let's go in that room over there so we can have some privacy."

Once they were settled with cups of coffee, Sam started asking questions. "OK, Mr. Franklin, Greg. Please tell me what you saw when you walked up to the bench in the park this morning."

Looking first at Janet, he began, "At first I was just mad because he was sleeping on my bench. I yelled, and then poked his arm. His arm fell, dangling off the bench. That's when I saw the blood, lots of blood. I ran to find a policeman. I didn't touch anything, but his arm that once."

The detective made notes as he continued. "Why were you in the park so early?"

Greg met the detective's eyes when he spoke. "I usually sleep in the park."

"Do you usually sleep on that same bench every night?" Detective Warren asked.

"Every night." Greg answered.

"How did it happen that you were not on the bench last night?"

Greg looked at Janet. "Dr. Janet asked me to sleep somewhere else. I ended up sleeping on the fire escape behind her building."

"Didn't she offer you a place to sleep?" Sam asked.

"Yes, she did, but I didn't feel right about staying with her." Greg didn't offer any more details.

"O.K., Dr. Leigh. Did someone tell you there would be trouble? Why did you tell Greg to sleep somewhere else?" They both waited for her answer.

"It's Janet." It wasn't easy to explain. "It was just a feeling I had."

"That's it. A feeling?"

"That's it."

"Do you get these feelings often?" He asked, not quite convinced.

"Occasionally."

Raising his eyebrows, Sam found it hard to believe there wasn't more to it than what she was telling him. "Where were you last night?"

"At home. I live at the Executive Plaza Apartments. The doorman saw me come in. I ordered a pizza about 8:00 and he walked up with the deliveryman. As you know, that is a high security building."

"Easy now. Don't get upset. I had to ask. We've had several murders of homeless people over the last few months. Greg, if we have more questions, can I contact you through Dr. Leigh?"

Greg looked at her for approval. "Yes."

"Great! Thank you for coming in this morning." Sam offered her his hand.

Janet liked how his hand felt in hers, strong and warm. They maintained eye contact for a moment before he released her hand. "Thank you. Nice to meet you, Detective."

Sam watched them leave, hoping he would get to see her again.

Out on the street, Janet hailed a cab. "Let's get back to my office." Janet didn't wait for a response.

Following her into the cab, Greg felt lost. "What happens now?"

Smiling, Janet surprised him with her answer. "That's up to you. Do you want to go back on the street, or do you want help to move on to something better?" They sat in silence for a long time as the cab driver fought through traffic.

Heaving a deep sigh, Greg made up his mind. "You remind me of my late wife. She was strong; she was my strength. We both taught at Harvard."

"Dr. Gregory Franklin. I think I read one of your papers when I was in college. Do you have family?" Janet was pleased with the direction of the conversation.

"A son. I've lost track of him or rather I have avoided

him. It's been about seven years." Greg looked down at his hands. "I guess time doesn't stand still, even when you are trying to shut out the world."

"We'll find him." She waited for an argument, and was pleased when none came.

Once they got back to the office, she asked Les if he would take Greg to her apartment for a shower. She gave him money for clothes, and a hair cut. Happy to be included in on one of her projects, Les enthusiastically jumped at the opportunity.

Greg found himself getting into another cab, and in minutes he was being ushered into Les' apartment. His apartment was farther away, but Les had decided it made more sense to go to his place. Handing Greg a terry cloth robe and a toothbrush, Les showed him where the bathroom was and told him to help himself to what he needed. After Les heard the shower running, he slipped into the bathroom and took Greg's old clothes. He was careful not to throw away anything in the pockets that Greg would want to keep, but the clothes went quickly into the trash downstairs.

From friends in neighboring apartments, Les found enough clothes for Greg to wear until they could buy something. Greg was a lot bigger built than Les. He knocked on the door and offered Greg the newer, cleaner clothes.

"Thank you." Greg appreciated the fact that Les had put his wallet and his few personal possessions on top of the pile of clean clothes. After being alone for so long, it made Greg uncomfortable being in someone else's home. It shamed him that he must accept charity, even from someone as nice as Les.

Les said he would fix them some lunch. "You come on out to the kitchen when you're ready."

Greg found shaving cream and a razor in the medicine cabinet, but there was just too much hair. Rummaging around, he found a pair of scissors and started cutting off his beard. About a half an hour later, he entered the kitchen slowly looking for Les.

"Wow!" Les looked Greg over from head to toe and would never have believed Greg had ever lived on the streets. "Sorry, but you look great. We'll find you some better clothes after we have something to eat." Les already had sandwiches ready on the table with a tall glass of milk for Greg. Les nibbled on his sandwich and sipped his juice.

Greg dug into his. "Mm, good! You have a nice place. I tried to clean up after myself in the bathroom."

Les told him not to worry about the bathroom. Greg finished his sandwich so he gave him the other half of his. "You can have it. I'm not that hungry today."

Greg started to object, but Les was already at the sink rinsing his plate. He left Greg to finish his lunch and went to clean up the bathroom. Surprisingly, Greg had indeed cleaned up all the hair, and wiped out the tub. Les used a disinfectant to scrub the tub and sink, but mostly out of habit. He brushed his teeth, and then went back to the kitchen. Greg was just finishing his milk.

"Great! Do you want to wash your hands or anything before we go?" Les didn't know if he was out of line. Some things just needed to be said.

"Yes, thank you." Greg thought Les was just being polite.

They walked together to the hair salon that Les preferred. It was only a couple blocks away. Greg was introduced to a very tall young man with spiky hair named Jam, who looked him over before asking him how short he would like it.

"I like it a little long in the back, over the collar. Not real short."

"Like a professor?" Jam asked.

Greg looked at Les and laughed. "Yes, like a professor."

"No problem. You've got great hair. My old man is almost bald." Jam kept on talking mostly to himself.

Les sat nearby and watched. Greg seemed quite amused by Jam, and Jam was doing a great job on Greg's hair. Janet would be very pleased and surprised.

About an hour later, they were window shopping, but Greg didn't like any of the stores they passed. "Too fancy."

Les led the way to one of the second hand stores he visited frequently for costumes for his plays. "Let's try this store. There are about five different stores I go to for costumes and props for my plays. If you don't like this one, we'll try another."

Greg followed him inside without argument this time. They found corduroy slacks, a plaid shirt, and a cardigan with patches on the sleeves. In Les's eyes the fit was not great, but Greg was happy. Les paid for the clothes, having the clerk put the borrowed clothes in a bag.

They made one more stop to buy some underclothes and two more shirts. Les wasn't sure where Greg was going, but he wanted him to have clean clothes.

In between appointments, Janet had also been busy. She had spoken to two professors at Harvard that remembered and admired Dr. Franklin. Not mentioning the hard times and the condition she had found him in, she just inquired if they knew where she could reach his son. Professor Allen referred her to Professor Gordon. Pleased that she was a friend of Dr. Franklin, he dispatched an assistant to find the address and phone number for her. Dr. Gordon did not seem surprised in the least or question the fact that Greg had lost touch with his son.

He was quick to inform her that he was also a member of the board of directors at the college. "Our next term starts in three weeks. That does not leave much time. He needs to be back on campus next Tuesday." Dr. Gordon rambled on.

"Are you offering him a chance to apply for a position?" Janet asked. She was quite pleased, but was not sure what

Greg would think.

"Better than that. You just tell him to be here next Tuesday. We've missed him, and we have an opening so that's that." He gave her the address and phone number of Greg's son.

"I'll have him call you." Janet thanked him, shaking her head in surprise.

"Not necessary. You just tell him to be here on Tuesday. Nice talking to you, Dr. Leigh." He hung up before she could respond.

Her last appointment of the day had just left when Les and Greg walked back into the office. Janet smiled warmly at Greg, and kissed him on the cheek. "I knew there was a handsome man under all that hair."

Greg's face flushed with embarrassment, but he was pleased with her response. Les earned a kiss on the cheek for a job well done.

"We are all going out to celebrate." She grabbed her purse and told Les to leave the files for the morning.

"I'm in. I don't have play practice until 7:00." Les winked at her. He had fun with Greg all afternoon, and was happy to go out with them.

There was a small Irish pub just down the street where Les and Janet had spent many evenings together. Finding an empty booth, they ordered drinks. They talked for a while and ordered dinner.

Deep into their conversation, none of them noticed the man who came into the door sometime later. The bartender pointed him in their direction. Dressed in jeans and blazer, he was a nice looking man with gray speckled dark hair and glasses. "Dad?"

Greg looked up in surprise. "William?" Getting up quickly, he pulled his son into his arms. They both wiped tears from their eyes. Remembering that they weren't alone, Greg turned to introduce his son to his new friends. "Dr. Janet Leigh. Les Bear. This is my son, William."

"Nice to meet you William. I'm so glad you could come right away." Janet shook his hand and greeted him warmly.

"Nothing would have stopped me. I left right after your call. Thank you." He was overwhelmed and grabbed his father for another hug.

Janet laughed and signaled for the waitress to bring a drink for William.

Greg was all smiles and would not leave William alone, patting his arm and hugging him. "Dr. Janet, you are one special lady. How will I ever thank you?"

"Seeing you happy is enough, but if you ever get a chance to help any of the others, please do."

Greg smiled. "You bet."

They had a nice dinner together. Not long after they finished their meal, William glanced at his watched. "I'm sorry, but we have to leave if we are going to catch the train home." He got up and offered his hand to Les. "Thank you for all that you did for my dad."

"The pleasure was all mine." Les offered his hand to each of them. "I'll miss you." He told Greg. "Please come and see me next time you are in the city."

"I'd like that." Greg moved to Janet and pulled her into his arms. "Thank you for not giving up on me. I'd be dead right now."

Janet gave Greg a kiss on the cheek. "Thank you for believing me. Oh, I forget to tell you. Do you remember a Dr. Gordon?"

"Yes, we've known each other a long time."

"Well, he gave me a message for you. He told me to tell you to be on campus on Tuesday morning."

"I don't understand."

"I gather from our conversation that he has a position for you at Harvard. I asked if he was offering you a chance to apply for a job, and he said that the position was already yours. He just assumed that you would be there to start work on Tuesday." Janet still couldn't believe their conversation.

"I guess I'll be there" Greg was surprised. "Tommy always was a little eccentric." He patted Janet on the cheek. "Take care of yourself."

"I will. You, too." Janet turned to William. "Good luck to both of you. Take care of him for us."

"Not to worry." William pulled Janet into his arms.

"Thank you," he whispered to her. "Thank you for everything," he said as he let her go. "Come on, Dad. We have a train to catch." Putting his arm around his dad, they walked out together, turning once to wave good-bye.

A few weeks later, they received a nice card from Greg. He was back teaching at Harvard, and had met a nice professor with pretty blue eyes. Greg told her about a food and blanket drive he had organized on campus. He promised her that this was just the beginning; he had many other projects planned to help the community. Greg thanked her again for her kindness, and told her he would find a way to repay that kindness tenfold.

Chapter Six

The more people she was able to help, the more Janet wanted to make a difference in the community. She started volunteering her time at nearby shelters to learn more about what it took to keep one running. When the shelters were in desperate need of food or repairs, Janet appealed to other businesses in the community for help.

To broaden her network of possible donors, Janet started accepting more invitations to social events. Les was her escort and was soon swept up in her cause as well. They each collected names, phone numbers and business cards from those they met hoping to appeal to these people in the future for contributions.

Les was actually better at it than Janet. He would flirt outrageously with debutantes and matrons alike. It was a harmless game since they all knew he was gay, but a very effective one. She began to believe that some of the invitations she received were extended just because the hostess knew Les would be her escort.

They made a good team. He could be counted on to help

where needed, as a volunteer, to run errands and to pick up donations. He could also be counted on to bring to her attention anyone who required special help.

Les helped Janet manage her time. They took their daily planners wherever they went, and Les often wrote appointments into hers. He sometimes had to consult her planner before scheduling office appointments for patients.

No matter how busy she was, Janet still went to the park at lunch time as much as possible. Going to the park to draw was relaxing and Janet needed that time away from her hectic schedule. When she hadn't been to the park for several days she also felt like she was neglecting her friends.

Chapter Seven

Her hair was more orange than red because she tinted it herself. She wore flowered skirts with ruffled blouses, a feather-trimmed jacket, long flowing bright scarves, and dangly earrings. Gwen made other bag ladies look dowdy. What set her apart from the others was more than her crazy clothes, she was meticulously clean.

Gwen spent her evenings going through the garbage in the best neighborhoods in town, looking for cast-off clothing she could sell to the second hand stores. For over ten years, Gwen had been covering the same neighborhoods. Some residents had met Gwen and found her charming. These were the houses that saved the best of their discarded clothing for Gwen, packing them neatly in bags or boxes. With the aid of a big red wagon, she hauled her treasures from shop to shop each morning for sale. One of the many shops that bought clothes from her offered Gwen a small room in the basement to stay.

Janet had met Gwen at the park one day. Once she started to sketch her, Gwen started telling Janet stories about

Broadway. She confided that she had been in a show once, in the chorus line. The second time they met, Gwen told Janet about her daughter.

"Does she live close by?"

Shaking her head, Gwen's face grew sad. "I don't know. My husband ran off with her when she was twelve. He didn't think the city or the theatre was a good place for Greta. He never liked the theatre or living in the city."

"Greta? Like Greta Garbo?"

"Yes, that's right, Greta Garbo." They moved around a lot and I eventually lost track of them."

"Are you still trying to find her?"

"No." Shrugging and shaking her head, Gwen admitted, "I gave up about ten years ago. I guess I just lost hope of ever seeing her again."

"How old would she be now?"

"Next month she will be 36."

Janet didn't ask any more questions, but hoped Gwen would keep talking about her daughter.

On the third occasion when they ran into each other again, Gwen was pleased to see her. "I came this way today, hoping I would see you again." She smiled warmly as Janet sat on the next bench so she could sketch her.

"It is nice to see you again, Gwen." Janet took a bite of her sandwich, and then opened her drawing pad. At first she took a few bites in between drawing, but the more she drew, the more she grew worried about Gwen. All she could see was Gwen on a gurney, and a paramedic covering her with a sheet. She couldn't see what would happen to her. The vision just wasn't clear. As the deeply lined face came to life on the paper, Janet tried to think how she could protect Gwen.

"When was the last time you went to a Broadway show?"

"At least ten years ago. That's when I quit working for one of the theatre companies."

"I can't remember the last time I had a chance to go to one; it has to be at least a year or so." Janet offered Gwen what was left of her lunch. She had lost interest in eating. "Why don't we walk down to the ticket office and see what tickets are available for tonight? We could go together? It would be fun. How about it?"

"But I work in the evenings, Deary."

"When is the last time you took a day off?"

"Can't remember, actually." Gwen studied Janet to see if she was truly serious.

"We could go to the hair dressers and to your favorite shop for just the right clothes. It would be fun." Without waiting for a reply, Janet took out her cell phone and left a message for Les to reschedule her afternoon appointments. "Let's go!"

Gwen felt a bit overwhelmed, being swept up in Janet's plans, but she fell in step with her. On the way to the ticket office, Janet asked a few questions. "Which shop is your favorite?"

"The Second Follies Shop."

"That is Les' favorite, too. He's my assistant and a dear friend. When he's not working for me, he directs and writes plays for young people. Most of his costumes are made from what he finds in that shop." Janet had gone to the shop with Les on several occasions. "Is that the same shop where you live?"

"Yes, the owner is very nice. He says he lets me stay there only so he can get first choice of my merchandise, but...." Gwen smiles at Janet. "I do help him out from time to time in the shop, mostly sorting clothes, and cleaning and steaming them before they go out for sale. I also clean the shop once a week. That was my idea, not his. I work in exchange for my room in the basement."

"Yes, Richard is very nice. He helps Les out with his plays sometimes. He's very good with ideas for props and scenery."

"Is Les your boyfriend?"

Janet smiled and shook her head. "No, Les is one of those theatre types. Let's say he is more like a girlfriend than a boyfriend."

"Oh." Gwen thought about that for a moment, and then her eyes grew bright. "Oh, I see."

At the ticket office, they decided to see 'Grease'. Because

of cancellations, they were lucky enough to get two cheap front row seats in the balcony. Janet insisted on paying, even though Gwen said she could afford her own. "My treat."

Now that they had purchased the tickets, Gwen was in awe that Janet really wanted to go to the theatre with her. "I don't know why you would want to go with an old bat like me, but I am so excited." She grinned at Janet.

Janet smiled as she led the way to her favorite hair salon. They went for the total package. Janet and Les often brought friends with them to the salon so the stylists were not surprised when they were introduced to Gwen. In fact, within a few minutes she had won Jam over with her charming ways. Taking his criticism of the condition of her hair in stride, she watched as he transformed her frizzy orange-red hair into an elegant rich red bob.

After a manicure, a facial, and make up, Gwen stared in the mirror in disbelief. Even when she had worked in the theatre all those years, she had never felt so pretty. "Would you pinch me deary, I think I'm dreaming."

Janet and everyone nearby laughed. "You look great!" They all confirmed Janet's opinion.

Sometime later, when they walked into the 'Second Follies Shop', Richard and his assistant Jeanne did a double take. "Gwen? Wow!"

Gwen was embarrassed by their reaction. "Thank you."

Janet spoke up to take the pressure off of Gwen. "Hello,

Richard, Jeanne. We are going to the theatre this evening, and need something really special to wear."

"Great to see you, Janet. I didn't know you two were friends." Richard asked about Les' latest project. Jeanne didn't hesitate a moment, and rushed out to find the perfect thing for Janet. There was a long sleek black dress that she really liked that would fit Janet's tall figure to perfection. She brought it to Janet with a black beaded scarf and a small beaded purse. "This would look great on you."

While Janet went to try the dress on, Jeanne took Gwen by the arm and led the way to a blue suit with beaded jacket and long skirt. It wasn't Gwen's usual style, but how often did Gwen go out with a doctor to the theatre. Gwen looked at Jeanne in doubt, but agreed to try the suit on.

Janet came out of the dressing room in time to see Gwen looking in the mirror. "That is perfect. You look great."

Gwen looked at Jeanne again to be sure. "I'll find you some shoes and a nice beaded bag." Gwen squeezed her hand in thanks, and then went to change.

While Jeanne rang up the sale and put their purchases in garment bags, Gwen went to her room and packed a few things to take with her. Janet had suggested she spend the night with her, and she had agreed mostly because she wanted to prolong her special evening out.

Janet was having a great time. Gwen was fun to be with and she really didn't get out much herself. She rushed Gwen to her apartment so they would have time to get something to eat before the show. To save them time later, she chose a nice Italian restaurant that was within a block of the theatre.

Since they left the apartment, Gwen had been very quiet. She worried that she would be out of place in the nice restaurant Janet was taking her to. Realizing her discomfort, Janet drew her arm through Gwen's as they walked to their table. Whispering, she tried to put her at ease, "This is an adventure. Who cares about what other people may think. You look great and we are going to have a great time."

Gwen flashed Janet a big grin. "You are quite right, deary. Thank you."

They did have a great time. Over supper, Gwen told Janet about her work in the theatre. Other than the one show where she had been in the chorus line, Gwen mostly worked as the wardrobe person for the lead characters in the play, keeping their costumes nice and helping them change costumes between scenes. "After a while, my type of work became a dinosaur, like me. Theatres decided it was too expensive to keep a full-time wardrobe person on staff. Many of the actors and dancers either had their own assistant to take care of their costumes or they chose to do it themselves." Gwen smiled in remembrance. "It was fun while it lasted."

"Most of the theatres had rooms upstairs where I could stay, so when I was out of work, I didn't have a place to live either. Not knowing where to go, I eventually ended up on the streets. One day when I was wandering around trying to figure out what to do next, I came across some great clothes one day in someone's garbage. That's how I got the idea for my business. Eventually, I asked Richard one day if I could use his bathroom to wash up. I really have a thing about being clean. A few days later, he offered me the room in the basement."

Janet admired Gwen's spunk. "You were one of the lucky ones. How long were you living on the streets?"

"I guess it was only a couple of months. Seemed like forever. It was terrible trying to find a safe place to sleep, and finding a place to clean up each day. People don't have very high opinions of bag ladies, and that is what I had become."

They didn't talk during the show. Their seats were great, and their full attention was on the stage. Gwen marveled at how easy the other people attending the show accepted her. Realizing that outwardly she looked no different than any of the others, it made sense that there was no reason for them to treat her different. This made her smile and she was able to relax and enjoy the evening to the fullest.

Later at Janet's apartment, they changed out of their fancy clothes and sat watching the news on TV. Gwen gasped when she saw a story about a store fire flash onto the screen and realized it was the 'Second Follies Shop'. Janet was equally surprised, and whispered quietly, "I didn't know about the fire."

Gwen studied Janet, and then glanced back at the TV. "What do you mean? I don't understand."

Watching the news, she glanced at Gwen as she tried to explain, "Sometimes when I draw a picture of someone I get these visions about the people and about things that are going to happen. Today, I sensed that you were in danger, but the picture I was seeing was not real clear. I didn't pick up on the fire."

"You did all of this just to protect me?"

"Yes, and no. It all started out that way. Once I got the idea to go to a show, the idea sort of sprouted wings. I had a great time this evening, didn't you?"

"I'm not complaining. It's just that…. Are you saying you thought I might have died tonight?"

Janet nodded.

"Wow!" Gwen sat back against the sofa feeling the reality strike her. "How often do your premonitions come true?"

Janet didn't say anything. She looked away to watch the news.

"You've never been wrong?"

Without looking at Gwen, she shook her head. She really felt uncomfortable talking about her gift. Not many could accept it easily.

Blowing out a breath, Gwen shook her head to clear the bad images that wanted to come to mind. "Well, my intuition told me to follow your lead. I guess God smiled on me the day we met in the park." Gwen walked over to Janet and hugged her. "Thank you!"

"You are quite welcome. Don't tell Richard; he might be a bit miffed that I didn't warn him." They both laughed to clear the air.

For a while they continued to watch the news, each deep in their own thoughts. Janet realized that they had watched Gwen's residence burn down, and that she was probably wondering where she would go.

She got up and brought her laptop back from the desk, sitting it on the coffee table. "Let's try to do some research." Once she was on the Internet, Janet found the website she liked best to look for people's addresses and phone numbers. "What is your daughter's full name? We'll try that first."

"Greta Garbo Jones."

Janet smiled as she typed in the name. "There shouldn't be many people with that name. If we don't get any results, we'll try the newspapers. If she got married, there might be an announcement."

As the results of the search popped up on the screen, they both looked at each other in surprise. Neither of them thought they would find Gwen's daughter that easy. Looking up the address, they found her to be at the same location as a shop, "Treasures". Neither Gwen nor Janet had ever heard of the shop before. Tears came to Gwen's eyes as she watched

Janet write down the information for her. "Would you like me to go with you tomorrow?"

Too overcome to speak, Gwen just nodded.

"Let's see if the shop has a website." Janet said as her fingers flew across the keyboard. "Wow, it can't be just a coincidence." Greta's shop was a second hand shop that specialized in costumes and vintage clothing."

"I can't believe that I've never been there before. I thought I knew every second hand shop in New York." Gwen said, once she found her voice again.

"Well, tomorrow will be a big day, bigger than today, so we had better get some sleep." Janet tidied up the living room, and then followed Gwen down the hall. As Gwen went into the guest room, she said, "Good Night."

"Good Night"

They were both up early the next morning. Janet fixed hot tea for both of them. From what ingredients she could find in her rather empty kitchen, Janet fixed them an omelet. Gwen offered to make the toast. They sat down at the small table in the kitchen to eat.

"Did you sleep O.K.?" Janet asked.

"Like a rock. I'm usually restless at night. Maybe it's because I feel so safe here."

"We also had a busy day yesterday. I had no problem falling asleep either."

Gwen was happy that she had met Janet that day. "I

bet you are a great psychiatrist. People feel at ease around you. I know I did from the moment we met. Thank you for everything you've done for me."

Janet just smiled and changed the subject. "I am so excited that we found your daughter. She must have moved back here to be close to you."

"Do you think so?" Gwen was a bit nervous about seeing her after so many years.

A few hours later, Gwen fiddled with her scarf as they rode the taxi towards her daughter's shop. Janet had helped her fix her hair. She didn't have a lot of choices on what to wear as all she had were the clothes she had quickly packed to go the Janet's, and what she had been wearing the day before, but she was neat and clean as always.

Janet reached over and gently squeezed her hand as they pulled up in front of the shop. "Let's go."

Greta was waiting on a customer when they entered the shop. Since she was busy, they had a chance to observe Greta before meeting her and to look around the charming shop. Janet could see the resemblance immediately, right down to their choice of clothing. Greta's hair was more auburn than red and she wore glasses, but she had the same build and facial features.

Gwen was very nervous. Janet tried to distract her by pointing out things around the shop and asking her opinion of a few dresses. Smiling at Janet, Gwen took a deep breath to collect herself. Giving her arm a little squeeze, Janet went back to looking around. Gwen followed her lead and was much more relaxed by the time Greta's customer left with her purchase.

"May I help you ladies with something special?" Greta said out of habit as she approached them.

Stopping in front of Gwen she looked at her as if she knew her. "Greta Garbo Jones." She held out her hand. "I'm sorry, I know you, but I can't remember your name."

"Guinevere Jones." She replied as she took her daughter's hand. Tears filled her eyes.

"Really? Mom? I've been hoping to find you." After a moment's hesitation she hugged Gwen.

"Oh, Greta, my baby." Gwen pulled her into her arms while both women began to cry.

Janet moved farther away to give them some privacy.

Pulling away from Greta, Gwen felt like she needed to defend her actions. "I tried for years to find you. I wrote letters to every address I could find. After a while, I didn't know where to look next." She touched her daughter's cheek. "I'm so sorry for everything I have missed in your life."

Greta shook her head. "Dad never gave me the letters. I found them all in a shoe box after he died two years ago. That's what brought me to the city; all the letters had a New York City return address. I have been trying to find you since I moved here. I checked with some of the theatres, but they didn't remember you." I majored in history in college and really like vintage clothing so I decided to open a shop here." She looked from Gwen to Janet. "How did you find me?"

Gwen pulled Janet closer. "Greta, this is the nicest lady you will ever meet. Dr. Janet Leigh, meet my daughter." They shook hands. "It is a long story, but I owe this lady my life. Last night we looked you up on the Internet and here we are."

"Nice to meet you, Dr. Leigh. Thank you for bringing us back together."

"Call me Janet. It is nice to meet you at last. You are all Gwen has talked about since we met. Do you have room for Gwen to stay with you? Her home burned down last night."

"You don't think I am going to let her out of my sight so soon after we finally get back together, do you? She can move in with me. We have a lot of catching up to do." Greta put her arm around Gwen, who was still dabbing at her eyes.

"Good. I'll leave the two of you alone to catch up on old times." Janet hugged Gwen. "Call me sometime so I know you are O.K."

Gwen nodded. "Thank you. I think you are my fairy godmother. This is so incredible."

Janet smiled. "I'm glad I could help you. Take care. Both of you."

"Thank you." Greta had her arm protectively around her

mother's shoulders.

With a wave, Janet left. Unable to flag down a cab, she was grateful for the walk and the time to think. A few blocks later she was able to flag down a cab and went into the office to catch up on work. She didn't feel like going back to her empty apartment.

Chapter Eight

While it was rewarding to be successful in helping people, her experiences also showed her how difficult it was not being able to help the many others she met on her forays into the park. When looking at the total number of homeless people in Manhattan, her successes had touched such a small percentage of those in need.

Janet began attending city council and city planning meetings hoping to find a way to help the homeless on a grander scale. One day she took a city map and marked the homeless shelters, soup kitchens, and counseling centers on it for her own reference. She noticed that there was one area of the city without a shelter, an area not far from Riverside Park.

Bringing the map with her to the next city counsel meeting, she showed the others her map. Next thing she knew, she had volunteered to oversea a project to open a new shelter.

Les loved the idea when she told him. He did not seem as overwhelmed by the project as she felt that first day. It would take months to complete the project even with Les' help.

Chapter Nine

One day during lunch hour she was on her way to an appointment across town. As her taxi drove slowly through traffic, Janet's eyes stopped on a young pregnant girl walking down the street. Walking down the sidewalk, she stopped suddenly grabbing her stomach. Traffic cleared and the cab lurched forward at a faster pace. At the next light, Janet jumped out and walked back to where she had last seen the girl.

Reaching the intersection without seeing her, Janet turned back the way she had come. Walking slowly, looking right and left to take in her surroundings in more detail, she found her not far from where she had last seen her sitting on the ground in an alley. Clutching her belly, her face was bathed in sweat.

"Hi! How long have the pains been coming?"

Looking up at her with fear in her eyes, the girl replied. "A few hours. They are getting stronger. Why does it hurt so much?"

Janet put her hand on the girl's stomach to try to judge

the position of the baby. "My name is Dr. Janet Leigh. What is your name?"

"Sheri Murphy. Ohh… Will you help me? I'm so scared."

"That's why I am here. You try to relax. I'll try getting a cab." She rushed back to the street. After several tries, she found a cabby that spoke English and was willing to help her get the girl in the car. "Thanks, my name is Dr. Janet Leigh."

"Ritchie."

"Sheri is over here in the alley. Hang on Sheri. I found someone to help us." Together they helped her up and slowly made their way to the cab.

Once they were inside, Janet started asking her questions to take her mind off the pain. "How long have you been on the streets?"

"Two months. They fired me at my waitress job once I got so big. I had to give up my room when I could no longer pay the rent."

"Is there anyone I can call for you?"

"No, my mom kicked me out."

"How about a boyfriend?"

Sheri would not look at Janet. "My stepfather…." She was too ashamed to finish.

They both heard Ritchie mutter, "Son of a bitch."

Janet kept her thoughts to herself.

"Oh…No." Sheri grabbed for Janet's hand as she rode through the pain. Taking a deep breath once it was over, Sheri continued to hold Janet's hand. "I hope it's a girl. I want to keep it."

"That's a very important decision." Janet admired her spunk. She would need it.

Ritchie pulled up to the emergency room exit, and ran inside for help. With Ritchie and Janet's help, Sheri was helped into a wheel chair and rushed inside.

Janet made a mental note of Ritchie's name off his license, wanting to thank him formally later. "Thanks!" She said as she handed him some cash and followed Sheri inside.

While waiting on news on Sheri, Janet called social services. She wanted to offer Sheri a place to stay, but thought it better to contact social services first since Sheri was under age. About an hour later, Eve Grayson arrived. She introduced herself and they discussed the alternatives for Sheri while they waited.

Ritchie came in asking for news. "Have you heard how she is? What will happen to Sheri and the baby?"

Janet told him they had no news yet and introduced him to Eve. "Ritchie helped me get Sheri to the hospital. I was just about ready to call for an ambulance, but it would have taken them a long time to get through lunch hour traffic. The other cabbies I stopped refused to help me."

Eve looked him over. "Janet has offered to help, but she isn't home during the day to help with the baby. I made a few phone calls before I got here, but I haven't found anyone who is willing to take both Sheri and the baby yet?"

Janet objected. "Sheri wants to keep the baby and I think we should give her that chance. Why can't they stay with me until you find another place for them? I could take a couple days off until she gets settled."

Eve laughed. "When was the last time you took a day off?" She recognized a workaholic when she saw one.

Ritchie spoke up and surprised both women. "My wife and I would love to have both of them stay with us."

"That's a very generous offer." Janet was pleasantly surprised at his interest in helping Sheri.

"My wife, Claire, and I haven't been able to have any kids of our own. We talked about adopting. Right now she is preparing the guest room. I think she would have been angry with me if I hadn't suggested it. I've never heard her more excited. I think it was meant to be."

Janet's eyes filled with tears. "I think you are right. Of all the cabbies in New York, you were the only one who stopped to help us."

Eve hesitated as she looked at Ritchie closer. Finally she made a judgment call. Opening her briefcase, she took out a form and started asking Ritchie questions, lots of questions.

Ritchie answered every one carefully. When they

finished, he asked her a couple questions. "How long will it take to check us out? Will Sheri be able to come home with us tomorrow? My wife is getting a room ready right now."

Eve smiled at his enthusiasm. "It's not all up to me. I'll check out the information you gave me, go visit your house, and talk to your wife. Then I will make a recommendation to my boss. We'll see if we can get you at least an approval for them to stay with you temporarily." She wondered if Ritchie sounded too good to be true. "You sure you don't have any skeletons in your closet that you haven't told me about? Anything you fail to tell us might eliminate you from getting approved."

Ritchie looked at her with concern. "I was wild in my youth, but I've been married 25 years, go to church every Sunday, don't drink or smoke, and I don't even like taking aspirin." Remembering his ball cap, he took it off and held it in both hands. "My wife's biggest disappointment was not being able to have babies. She is really looking forward to this. I told her not to count on it, but we really want this chance to help both Sheri and the baby."

Smiling at him, Eve knew he would do whatever he could to make it work. "Well, let me go make some phone calls. I'll call you later this evening." Picking up her briefcase she turned to Janet. "Nice meeting you."

Janet shook her hand. "Let me know what I can do to help."

They watched her leave, and then sat back down to wait.

A few moments later a nurse came out to tell them that Sheri had a healthy little girl, a little small, but still healthy. A nurse was taking the baby out as they walked into the room.

"Did you see her?" Sheri asked the minute they entered the room. "Isn't she great?" She was so relieved that the ordeal was over and the baby was fine. "Thank you so much for helping me and waiting. It helped me just knowing that I had someone here with me. I tried to get them to let you in with me, but they said only family could come in."

"You have a wonderful little girl." Janet gave Sheri a hug.

Ritchie moved closer on the other side of the bed. "She looks like you." A little nervous about Sheri's reaction, he hesitated.

Sheri held out her arms for a hug. He smiled and gently folded her into his big arms. "The nurse said we should be able to take you home the day after tomorrow."

Looking into his eyes, she hoped he was serious. "Home?"

"Would you consider coming to live with my wife, Claire, and I? We don't have any kids, and we would really like having you stay in our home." Ritchie looked at her expectantly.

64

Sheri didn't know much about Ritchie, but he seemed nice. He was slightly plump, but neat and clean with a kind face.

Janet didn't blame the girl for being cautious. "Social services, Eve Grayson, is checking out Ritchie and his wife. I offered to let you come and stay with me, but Eve thought you needed someone that was home more to help with the baby. What would you like to do?"

Ritchie stood quietly waiting for her to say something. He took his cap off his balding head and fiddled with it. Sheri thought he looked like someone's uncle. Smiling, she held out her hand to him. "O.K., but just for a few days."

Janet understood her need to be independent. "Call me tomorrow and I'll help you any way I can. Eve and I can help you get some help through local agencies." She handed her a business card. "Since you are seventeen, you should be able to sign up for some public aid programs to help you with food and medical assistance until you get a job. You do have some options."

Janet thought it was time for her to go. She gently squeezed Sheri's hand. "We should let you get some rest."

Ritchie took the hint. "I'd better go so I can help Claire fix you a room. See you tomorrow."

Sheri called Janet the next morning to say Eve had stopped by and brought the forms for the programs that Janet had mentioned. "I've decided to stay with Claire and Ritchie for a few days until I can find a place of my own. "

Janet thought Ritchie could be trusted and hoped Clair was as nice. "All you have to do is call me if you want to leave or need anything."

A few days later, she went to visit them. Sheri had called Janet the day before, begging her to come and visit. Sheri was recovering quickly, both emotionally and physically with all the loving care from Claire and Ritchie.

"You're here! I'm so glad you came." Sheri hugged Janet.

"You look good. How's the baby?"

Sheri pulled Janet into her room to see the sleeping baby in a crib in the corner. "Do you want to hold her?" She whispered.

"No, let her sleep. I'll just take a peak." Janet smoothed the blanket over the baby. "Is she good?"

"An angel. Hardly ever fusses unless she really has something to complain about." Ritchie is bringing me a rocking chair tonight. I'll be able to sit with her at night and rock her while I feed her."

"What did you name her?" Janet looked on as Sheri touched her baby's cheek.

"Janet Leigh Murphy."

Janet looked at Sheri to see if she was serious. "Really?" Tears stung her eyes as she looked down at her namesake.

"Claire arranged for the christening next Sunday. I want

you to be her Godmother. O.K.?" Sheri really wanted Janet to be a part of her new family.

"What about Ritchie and Claire?"

"They are really great, more like a mom and dad to me than my real ones." She paused. "I want you to be my baby's Godmother. She needs someone she can aspire to be like when she grows up."

"I'd be honored." Reaching down into the crib, she touched the baby's cheek.

Sheri didn't pause for more than a minute. "I've decided to stay here until I graduate. By then I'll be 18 and I can decide where I want to live. It's so cool. Claire says she will babysit so I can go back to school on Monday. She even worked it out with the teachers and the principal so I can make up all the work I've missed in time to graduate."

The baby fussed a little sucking on her tiny fist. "Little Janey is always hungry." Picking up the baby, she handed her to Janet.

"My dad always called me Janey." The baby continued to suck on her fist. When Janet shifted the baby's position, she started looking for her milk source. Janet decided this was a definite sign she needed to go back to her mom. "I'd better go so that you can feed her. I'll talk to you later this week." Janet picked up her purse to go.

"The day I met you and Ritchie was the luckiest day of my life."

"It helped that I was able to flag down the nicest cabbie in New York." They hugged each other with the baby in between.

Janet attended the christening and later that year she attended Sheri's graduation.

Chapter Ten

After her successes or failures, Janet would often venture to a different section of the park. One fall day she found a stone wall to sit on. The sidewalk curved down and angled away from where she sat in two directions.

A young man, maybe 16 or 17, came along on his skateboard. Up and down, around and around he went trying out different techniques. After awhile he noticed Janet sketching and went to sit beside her. "Hi!" Taking a bite of an apple he fished out of his backpack, he glanced at what Janet was doing and then at the view below.

"Hello. You are pretty good on that thing. I would break my neck, especially going down hill." Janet greeted him. "Would you like half my sandwich? I never eat all of it."

Shrugging, he took the bag from her. "Why do you pack so much if you never eat all of it?"

"Then, I wouldn't have anything to give away."

Giving her a typical confused teenager look, he finally laughed. He started eating the sandwich.

"Why aren't you in school?"

"I work afternoons and evenings at one of the warehouses

not far from here. The school lets me out early to work. It's one of those special programs." He explained in his own way.

Janet thought she had some idea where the warehouses were he was talking about. Turning the page, she began another drawing. This one held only the boy's image. Keeping the sketch simple without a lot of detail, she signed it and tore it out for him. "Maybe we will run into each other again soon. It's time for me to go back to work.

Looking at her sketch in amazement, he said. "You make it look so easy."

"My name is Janet Leigh." She offered him her hand.

Smiling warmly, he shook her hand. "Alex Drumhill. Thanks! See you around."

A few days later, she ran into him again. "Hi! My mom about flipped when I gave her your sketch. She made you some cookies, but I didn't see you. They were good." He smiled at her mischievously.

Making a face at him, Janet laughed. "It's nice to see you, Alex." Nodding towards her forgotten lunch, she sketched him as he ate. She could see that he was a good boy, one his mother could be proud of. He was hard working and got along well with the people he worked with. Suddenly, it was as if a cold wind blew through the park, the feeling of danger came that quickly. "How late do you usually work?"

"Eight, nine, or ten, depends on how many trucks they

expect."

"Do they ever ask you to work into the early hours of the morning?"

"Twice. Mom doesn't like it, because I usually ditch school the next day. It wipes me out."

"Would you promise me something?"

Alex shrugged.

"Don't work past eleven tonight. There's going to be trouble around midnight.

"What kind of trouble?"

"The warehouse will be robbed by a gang, a very dangerous gang."

He watched her for a few minutes, looking to see how serious she was. "Don't worry. I promised my mom I'd be home at a decent hour tonight. I have a test tomorrow."

"Good. You be careful on the streets tonight." She worriedly told him as she packed up to leave. "Maybe I'll see you tomorrow."

"Sure. Thanks!"

That was the last time she saw him. Someone didn't show up to work so Alex's boss offered him double time if he would stay late. He did remember her warning, but soon forgot it. The money was too appealing. Alex thought of the nice birthday present he could buy his mom with the money.

A local gang came running in just after midnight. Alex

and his coworker were quickly killed when they tried to run away. Janet had called in an anonymous tip to the police, but they didn't place much importance on the call and arrived too late to help the boys or to catch who did it. She went to the funeral a few days later.

Chapter Eleven

As the days became cooler and shorter, Janet started her annual blanket drive. She appealed to the newspaper and they promised to run a notice several times each week. Janet had been instrumental in starting the first blanket drive five years ago, and the community relied upon her to organize the drive each year.

Once the newspapers began publicizing the blanket drive, other charitable organizations always helped with the collection and distribution. Churches in the area put out donation boxes. So did the American Legion, the Elks Club, some banks, and a few department stores.

Each year she bought a large number herself and started distributing them when the nights started falling below freezing. She would take a few each day with her to the park. A few days she asked Les to take a large number in his car to a location where she had seen a large amount of homeless that she thought might need them.

Some of the schools also started blanket drives, and Les volunteered to go and pick them up. Their goal was to collect the blankets and get them distributed in time for

73

the majority of the blankets to be distributed on Christmas Eve. Special dinners were served in many locations for the homeless at the shelters, soup kitchens, and many churches. This was a great opportunity to offer blankets. Other agencies brought donated jackets, gloves, hats, and other clothing to pass out.

Chapter Twelve

On one particularly cold day, she met a middle-aged man who was dressed in denim blue from head to toe - jeans, jacket, chambray shirt, and even boots and hat. He wore a red kerchief round his neck. She introduced herself to him, but he just sat there as if she had not spoken. Because he would sit and stare at the unknown for hours at a time, he was a good subject to draw. Occasionally, he would glance in her general direction for just a moment. When she offered him a blanket, he continued to stare straight ahead.

The second time she saw him, he had the blanket with him. She set her sack lunch on the bench where he sat, and then took a seat on the next bench. Either hunger or curiosity drew him to the lunch bag. He picked through the contents and ate what appealed to him most, leaving the rest. After sitting near him a few times, Janet learned what he liked best. One day she packed her lunch with everything she thought he preferred: pastrami and Swiss cheese on rye bread, green grapes, a gala apple, and peanut butter crackers. He rewarded her with a big smile that lit up his eyes, and then went back to staring blankly straight ahead.

When trying to analyze him, she came up with a few theories. Maybe he was a deep thinker, someone really smart that was trying to figure out the solutions to the many problems of the world or maybe he was so withdrawn into his own private world that he only emerged when he wanted to. At least she had reached him.

His chiseled features were a challenge to draw. What puzzled her most was that she felt nothing while drawing him, no images from his past or future or even a glimpse into his personality. After a couple weeks, she didn't know any more about him than she did when she first met him, except for what he liked to eat.

A few days later, she was sitting on a bench sketching some seagulls, when a terrible feeling hit her. Jumping up, she walked quickly down the paths where she had seen him before, desperately hoping to find him. A police officer that passed her noticed that she was behaving oddly and turned around to catch up with her. "Is there something I can help you with?" He offered.

"Do you walk the area of park everyday?" She asked putting her hand on his arm.

"Usually, unless I get called away. Why?"

Janet introduced herself so he might take her more seriously. She described the denim dressed man to the officer. "Have you seen him today?"

"No, not today."

"He's in trouble. Something has happened to him. I just know it."

The officer remembered what the nanny had told him after the drive by at the theatre. "So this was the lady who tried to help others," he thought as he watched her.

"Let's try the tunnel over there. I've seen him sleeping in there a few times." As they neared the tunnel, the officer motioned for her to stay behind him. He caught a glimpse of blue fabric. "Wait here. I'll check it out." He wanted to spare her any unpleasantness.

In her mind, Janet already knew what he would find. She did not wait, but followed him closely. They found him lying in an expanding pool of blood. "Oh, it looks bad." She reached forward to check his pulse. "He's still alive."

The officer called for an ambulance while Janet looked over her blue friend. It was obvious that the stabbing had happened not long before they arrived.

"Hang on. You have to hang on until help gets here." She kept talking to him. "I need something to use for a bandage." Janet looked pleadingly at the officer. She had already used the tissues and napkins she could find, but they were really useless. If she were wearing a suit, she would have taken off her blouse, but today she was wearing a dress.

Hesitating only a moment, the officer stripped off his uniform shirt and flack jacket. He took off his underwear shirt and handed it to Janet along with his pocketknife. Cutting and tearing the shirt into sections, Janet began putting pressure on the two stab wounds. Before the officer could finish buttoning his shirt again, she pulled him down next to her to help put pressure on one of the bandages.

Two paramedics arrived by way of the road that passed over the tunnel, and came running down the hill. Once they moved in, Janet stepped back out of the way as did the officer. "Does anyone know his name?" One of the paramedics asked.

Janet shook her head and looked at the officer. "He's never spoken to me. I always wondered if he had a physical problem that kept him from speaking."

The officer spoke up. "I think I heard one of the other homeless call him Joe, but that is probably just a nickname because no one knows his name.

"Hey, Joe. You've got to hang on." The paramedic talked to him as she worked. To her partner she said, "Pulse is getting weaker." They started an I.V. and oxygen, and then placed him on the cart.

Once Joe was strapped on, they asked the officer for help getting him up the hill and into the ambulance. "O.K., let's go.

"I'll follow you over. Doc, do you want to ride with me?"

Janet agreed to go, mostly for her own peace of mind.

Halfway to the hospital, the ambulance pulled over. Joe had crashed. One paramedic was administering CPR, the other used the paddles several times without success. Janet offered to help, but there was little else any of them could do for Joe.

As the officer drove her back to her office, Janet kept thinking about Joe. "I really hate the thought of him being buried without a name. Maybe there is someone who cares about him, who would see that the proper arrangements would be made. Isn't there some way to run his fingerprints? Maybe he was in the military?" Her eyes pleaded with the officer.

Patting her on the shoulder, he promised. "I'll do my best to find out who he was."

After thanking him, Janet got out and ran into her office. Les took one look at her soiled clothes and sad face and knew without asking that Janet's latest efforts to help were not rewarded with successful. "You go freshen up. I'll ask your next appointment to wait. Give me ten minutes and I'll be back with some clean clothes from your apartment."

Janet just nodded. The tears began to fall as soon as she shut the door. If she had been able to see ahead of time what would happen, she might have been able to save him. When she did pick up on his distress, it was like he was mentally appealing to her for help. Most unusual. Taking a deep breath, she looked into the mirror. After washing her face, she felt better. At least she had tried to help him.

By the time Les got back, Janet had washed up and changed her panty hose. She always kept spares at the office. Slipping on the clean dress he brought her, she turned so he could zip her up. She kissed him on the cheek then gave him a hug. "Thanks!"

At the end of the day, Officer Duncan called her. "His name is Henry William James. You were right, he was in the military. We found a brother who will be here tomorrow."

"Thank you. In some small way that is a relief."

"You were probably the best friend Henry ever had."

"Thanks!" Janet replied.

"How did you know he was hurt?" He asked.

"Just a feeling I had."

Officer Duncan did not question her further. "I am real pleased to have met you, Doc."

"Thank you. I hope we meet again under better circumstances."

Chapter Thirteen

Janet's work was interesting because she like helping people. Using her gift carefully, she used these insights to draw her patients out in conversation while taking care not to mention the secrets they may never tell her. Being able to gain more knowledge of their problems often helped her decide the best methods to use for therapy.

Teenagers were her favorite to work with. One day a week she visited one of the local high schools, rotating to different schools. Teachers would encourage troubled students to take time to see her. Sometimes she would gain their trust, others weren't so easy.

Because she was always sketching as they talked, her drawings were one way to capture the student's interest and a good way to open up a conversation. There were a few that would sit for the whole hour saying next to nothing, and then get up and leave. It was sad because these were the ones who needed help the most and they never came back after the first time.

On one visit, Janet met a cute 16-year old blonde girl

named Ashley Jansen. Very thin and very quiet, Ashley was a good student, but her teacher was concerned that she may be having trouble at home. At first she was reluctant to talk. What really interested her was Janet's drawing. Sitting closer to her, Janet let her watch as she finished her sketch. Turning the page, she tore out a blank sheet and gave it to Ashley with a pencil. They spent most of their remaining time perfecting Ashley's drawing techniques. She drew a still life with Janet's coffee mug, a pencil holder, a stapler, and a tape dispenser. Ashley smiled at Janet, which was like turning on a bright light on her somber face.

"Do you ever have time after school? I'd like to set up a regular time to meet each week."

Deeply worried, the girl's attitude changed in a moment. "I'm afraid to tell my mom or her boyfriend, especially him."

Janet didn't ask the many questions that came to mind. "How about if you say you are going to free art lessons once a week? No pressure. You think about it and call me." Janet gave Ashley her business card and the drawings. "I hope we see each other again soon."

"Thank you." Ashley smiled again, a sadder smile.

A few days later Ashley called her office. Les knew Janet was almost done with her client so he stalled for time by asking which school she attended. He was working on a stage show at her school and tried to recruit her to help with props. She didn't say no, just that she would think about it. When he saw the client leaving Janet's office, he transferred the call.

"Hi! Ashley. I'm glad you called."

"Dr. Janet. The art lesson thing worked. When can we get together?"

"Do you want to come here to my office or would you feel more comfortable meeting at the library or Riverside Park?"

"There would be a lot to draw in the park." She sounded hopeful.

Janet called Les into her office and they figured out the trains she would have to take. "Let's meet at the fountain. See you tomorrow."

"Thank you. I think this will be fun." Ashley seemed to be looking forward to their meeting.

After Janet hung up, they both sat still thinking about the girl. Les finally spoke. "I can sense that this girl really needs help. Let me know if there is anything I can do."

"I will, thanks." Janet smiled as he walked out. They made a good team.

At least the weather was nice the next day. Janet worried that they hadn't made additional plans in case of bad weather. Ashley arrived shortly after, greeting her with a smile and a wave. They found a bench under a tree that overlooked a large area of the park. It was a pretty time of the year with all of the leaves turning bright colors, even if most of them were already on the ground.

Janet gave Ashley her own sketchpad and some pencils. Unsure at first of what to draw, she sat quietly looking for a good subject. They could see a businessman under a tree nearby who was napping. Sitting on his briefcase, he had his head on his folded arms, which were resting on his bent knees. His newspaper was still in one hand, unopened. Janet just had to draw him.

Ashley watched her draw for a few minutes before trying it herself. From time to time she would glance at Janet's then back at her own. Their subject conveniently continued his nap for at least a half an hour. Something must have startled him, because he suddenly sat up and looked at his watch before walking briskly away.

Janet and Ashley shared a smile. "I like coming here and watching people." Janet told her. Using Ashley's drawing, Janet showed her some different techniques she could use. Ashley tried them out with some coaching from Janet. She did not push the girl to talk that first day.

A week later they met at the same place, but walked to a different area where they could sit in the fading sun for warmth. This gave Ashley a chance to draw people in a different setting. They each chose a different subject. Janet helped Ashley from time to time while finishing her own sketch.

Sitting her own sketchpad aside, Janet opened the conversation. She wasn't sure if Ashley was ready to talk. "How long has your mom's boyfriend lived with the two of you?"

"Hank owns part of the club where my mom was working. It's been about three years since he first started staying over night. She doesn't love him or anything like that. I think she is afraid of him."

"Your mom's name is Beth?" Janet asked quietly. She had looked over Ashley's school file.

Ashley nodded, replying in the same quiet manner. "After the first year things got worse. He was mean to her. Mostly he shouted, but then he started hitting her."

Janet patted her hand, but said nothing hoping she would continue.

"About the same time he became abusive, my mom started to drink. The more he hit her the more she drank. Two weeks ago, they fired her for always being late for work. Hank came home and called her all kinds of names, telling her she was worthless. After that night, she is usually passed out by the time I get home from school."

Ashley sketched a little, and then looked back at Janet. "Hank hits her now sometimes to try to wake her up. She just curls into the fetus position and covers her head."

Filling in some detail on her drawing, Ashley did not say anything for several minutes. "I tried to stop him once. That

85

was a big mistake. I think he forgot about me until then."

She continued to draw, but wouldn't look up at Janet. "He bought me candy, and a big ugly purse. I thanked him and went to my room. After that I tried to make myself as invisible as possible. I'd stay in my room and try to come out only when I thought he had left or went to bed. It was a blessing when he passed out."

Ashley paused. Janet sketched the same thing Ashley was drawing to give her some pointers. She didn't push Ashley to talk. It was several minutes before she continued.

"About two weeks ago, Hank was home when I got home. Mom was having a good day and fixed us all a nice supper. Hank even complimented her cooking. It was nice. I smiled at Mom and she gave me a nervous smile back."

"Then she started drinking again while doing dishes. She put it in a coffee cup like she had to hide it. Hank started touching her and I left the room. Later I heard yelling and the door slam when he left."

Ashley put the drawing down. "He came into my room the next morning. It was after 3:00, because I remember hearing him come in the door and looking at the clock.

"I must have gone back to sleep, because I didn't hear the door to my room open. He threw back the covers, and then pushed my nightgown up high enough so he could see my breasts." Ashley looked at the ground as she spoke. "He squeezed them hard, before sucking and biting them.

I cried out, because it hurt. He must have been afraid my mom would hear, because he told me to keep quiet." Ashley started to cry.

"Hank threw my nightgown over my face. I could feel him touching me. He pushed my legs apart and I struggled to get away. After tearing off my underwear, he pushed himself inside me. When I yelled "No", he hit me. After that I just laid there and cried."

Janet spoke. "When was that?"

Ashley shook her head. "Over three weeks ago."

"Is he still coming into your room?" Janet asked.

"Almost every night. I tried wearing a sweatsuit to bed the next night. That made him really angry. He ripped it off, and then made me lay on my stomach on the bed. He took off his belt and beat me with it. Next thing I knew he was entering me from behind."

Ashley started sobbing. Janet put her arm around her shoulders.

"Every night he has some new perversion he wants to try. It's better if I don't fight him. At least he doesn't hit me as much."

They sat a long time in silence. Janet didn't trust her self to speak for several minutes, her anger was that great. Finally she began. "It is not right what he is doing to you. Your mother is in no shape to protect you. You cannot go back home."

"Where will I go?"

Janet was determined to keep Ashley out of the system if she could. "Don't worry. You can stay with me tonight unless you have someone else. Do you have anyone else, a relative or a family friend?" Janet pulled out her cell phone and address book.

"Only Judy Wentz, my teacher." Ashley volunteered.

"Good suggestion. She has a wonderful reputation. Social services will love her as first choice." Janet began making phone calls. Her first call was to Eve Grayson, the social worker that had helped Sheri. "Eve. How are you?" Janet explained the circumstances, and mentioned Judy's name. "Are you available to meet us at the E.R. at Mount Sinai Hospital?" Janet was silent, while she listened to Eve. "O.K, see you there."

Ashley had stopped crying and was listening to her conversation. "Why do we have to go to the hospital?"

"It's a formality." Janet didn't want to alarm Ashley. "What he did to you is considered to be rape. We need to see if we can collect any evidence against him. It may be too late, but we have to try." Ashley's eyes grew wary. "It will be O.K. I'll stay with you. Did you shower or bathe after he came into your room last night?"

Shaking her head, she began to cry again. "No, Hank was in the bathroom when I got up. So, I got dressed real fast and ran out of the house so I wouldn't have to talk to him."

"They are able to gather more evidence, if you don't bathe first." Janet gathered her things and Ashley did the same. "Come on. We'll take a cab."

Ashley was frightened and very quiet on the ride over. They were met in the waiting room by a policewoman who introduced herself as Officer Ames, and a few minutes later by Eve Grayson and Judy Wentz. Judy sat on the other side of Ashley while they waited. Both women were allowed to go with Ashley into the examining room. Judy held Ashley's hand while Janet explained the procedure. Once the doctor came in, Ashley grabbed Janet's hand, too. Lucky for her, he was nice and had a gentle manner. After examining her and collecting samples, they took a few photographs to show the tears from forced entry and the many bruises that covered her thighs. It was over quickly and not as difficult as Ashley had imagined.

Judy stayed with her and helped her get dressed. Janet went outside with Eve and Officer Ames to hear the doctor's report. "These cases make me really angry. To make such a sweet girl see such ugliness." The doctor paused to control his anger. He had a daughter about the same age. "We were able to collect a lot of evidence. If you can get a sample of this guy's DNA, I think you have a case that will send this bastard to jail. I wish they would lock people like that up and throw away the key."

"Thank you, Doctor." Officer Ames took the copies of

the report from the nurse.

Still angry, he nodded and left to see the next patient.

Asking Janet and Eve a few questions, Officer Ames finished filling out her report. Picking up the evidence bags from the nurse, she left to arrange for Hank to be picked up.

With Eve's permission, Judy asked Ashley to go home with her. It would be a temporary arrangement until the official approval of Judy as Ashley's foster parent and a court custody hearing. Judy was young when her husband died. They didn't have any children and she had never remarried. She was Assistant Principal at the school and Eve could see no problem with the court giving the arrangement their blessing. Judy and Ashley left together in a cab.

Eve talked Janet into going with her to Beth's apartment. They would wait until the police left before going upstairs. When they arrived, Hank was being hauled downstairs and into a police car. He was struggling and yelling obscenities at the officers. Officer Ames gave them a satisfied smile before getting in her car to take him to the station.

Finding the door open, they knocked and entered. Another officer was trying to talk to Beth, but she was intoxicated and having trouble staying awake. Janet went into the kitchen to make coffee. Eve and the officer half carried Beth into the shower and turned the cold water on her.

A few minutes later dressed in a sweat suit, Beth sat on the couch and watched Eve and Janet over the top of her coffee cup. "What's going on? Where did they take Hank? Where's Ashley?"

Eve answered her questions. "Hank has been crawling into you daughter's bed at night."

"Nooo, did he hurt her? Did he…?" Beth realized what Eve was saying and started to cry. Sobering up, she started to act more like a concerned mother. "Is she O.K.? Did he hurt her?"

Janet let Eve answer her. "She will be O.K. The emotional scars take longer to heal."

She started to cry. "Can you lock him away for good? If he gets out, he'll come back to hurt us?

"You will have to testify against him." Eve told her.

"When is Ashley coming home?" Beth asked.

"We found her a safe place to stay for a while." Eve watched Beth to make sure she understood what she was telling her.

"Where is she?"

"She's staying with Judy Wentz for a while."

"Her teacher? She's a good woman." Beth seemed happy with their choice of a temporary guardian. "When can she come back?"

"I think that is up to you and the courts."

Sighing, Beth got up and saw the messy apartment as the others were probably seeing it.

"Can you get her into a treatment center?" Janet asked.

Eve replied. "I might be able to find an opening in a few days, but you have to stay sober." Beth stopped what she was doing for a moment. "I know a place that takes people who want to dry out based upon the courts recommendations. They take in a lot of mothers like you that are in jeopardy of losing the custody of their children. This place will only give you one chance. If you mess up or try to leave, you won't be able to go back."

"I promise I won't drink any more. I'll clean up this place and make it nice for Ashley when she comes home." Beth started stacking newspapers, and gathering empty beer bottles, fast food wrappers, plates and cups that were scattered about.

"I think it would be better if you went to stay with someone else for a while. Do you have a friend that would help you?" Eve thought a change in environment would be good.

"No, I don't have anywhere else to go. I don't want to go to a shelter. They are full of drunks."

Janet agreed with Eve that it would be better if Beth left for a while. "How about the battered women's shelter? Do they have any openings?"

Eve shook her head. "I have two cases right now that I couldn't find a place for." She turned back to Beth who had taken an armload of dirty dishes to the kitchen. "Beth, are you sure you will be alright here? How about a neighbor?"

Beth came back into the room to get the stack of newspapers. "No, they are all afraid of Hank. He made it quite clear that he didn't want any of them interfering with our business. I'll be fine."

Eve couldn't think of another place for Beth to go. As long as Hank was behind bars she would be safe. She still hated leaving her alone. Beth promised to come to her office the next day and to call in everyday. Her phone wasn't working, but there was a pay phone downstairs.

Beth walked them to the door. "Tell Ashley that I love her and that I'm sorry. Somehow saying I'm sorry doesn't sound like much. What a fool I've been." Offering her hand to each of them, Beth thanked them.

As they walked downstairs, Janet expressed concern about keeping Hank in jail. If he got out on bail, Beth's safety could be in jeopardy. Eve promised to talk to Officer Ames.

It took two days for the approval of Judy as Ashley's foster parent. A court date for the custody hearing was set for the next Thursday. Beth was true to her word and called Eve everyday. Eve went to visit her once to see how she was doing and was pleased with her progress. Beth was very nervous and shaky, but promised she would not drink ever again.

Hank was arraigned and bail was set at $100,000. After several days Hank was able to talk his bookie into helping him with the bail by putting up his share of the bar as collateral. On the Wednesday after his arrest, he walked out of the police station. He asked his bookie to drop him off at Beth's apartment.

Officer Ames did not hear about Hank's release until about an hour later. With her partner, she took a squad car and rushed over to Beth's. Pulling up in front of the building, they got out of the car and heard a scream. Looking up, they were just in time to see Hank throw Beth out of the apartment window. Officer Ames called it in and rushed to check Beth's condition while her partner rushed upstairs. Beth's bent and broken body lay lifeless. She could not find a pulse.

Hearing shouting coming from the broken window upstairs, she ran to help her partner subdue Hank. Her partner was on the floor unconscious. Blood ran from the gash in his head where Hank struck him. Hank had the other officer's gun and was waving it around. Panic shone in his eyes as the reality of what he had done was sinking in. When he saw Officer Ames, he pointed the gun at her. "Stay away or I'll shoot."

"Put the gun down and we'll go down to the station and talk about all of this." She tried futilely.

"No way." A shot hit the doorframe as she peeked around the door.

"Drop it now." She warned him.

Another shot bounced off the doorframe. Staying out in

the hall, she waited for Hank to come out or show himself. When the door opened, she fired. She hit him in the shoulder. Hank fell and she kicked the gun away. Acting quickly, she rolled him over and put on the handcuffs. Two more officers were coming up the stairs and half carried the belligerent Hank down to the squad car.

Officer Ames ran into the apartment to check on her partner. He was trying to sit up. She found him a towel to hold to his head, and helped him slowly down the stairs. As if in autopilot, she called into the office to talk to the chief while she drove Officer Williams to the hospital.

Later that day, Officer Ames came to Janet's office. Les asked her to wait a few minutes until Janet's patient left. When Les told her she could go in, she suddenly felt foolish for bothering Janet. Knocking on the door, she asked. "Do you have time to talk?"

Janet was just hanging up the phone. "Come on in." Janet stood up and offered the officer a chair. "Eve called me. Are you O.K.? What was your first name?"

"Mirabelle." That was all she could manage before she started to cry. After a few minutes, she took a deep breath and tried to gain control. Janet sat the box of tissues where she could reach it. "I'm sorry. I just had to talk to someone. Everyone thinks I am strong, but this really hit me. If I'd been there just a few minutes sooner or if we had posted an officer there to watch Beth's apartment, she may still be alive."

Janet understood the helpless feeling that remained after a tragic event. "You got there as soon as you could, right?"

Mirabelle nodded.

"The system failed Beth, not you. We just have too many people that need help, and some people fall between the cracks. All we can do is try our hardest to make the system work for those that need it. Sometimes we are successful and other times we aren't. I know that this doesn't help how you feel right now, but you cannot put the blame on yourself."

Mirabelle nodded again. "You are right. I did get to shoot that son-of-a-..., that is some concession I guess." Trying to smile, she stood up and offered her hand to Janet. "It was really great of you to take time to see me. I feel a little better. I admire your work with the homeless."

"I do what I can. Sometimes I can make a difference and sometimes their fate has already been determined and nothing I do can change that. I'm sure it is the same with your job, you make a difference when you can." Janet walked her to the door.

"I don't do much volunteer work, but I think after today that may change. Thanks, again." Officer Ames put on her cap, nodding to the people waiting.

Janet called the school and had Judy Wentz paged. Janet told her about Beth and Hank. "Eve suggested I call you. I wanted to tell you before the incident hit the news and someone else told Ashley." Janet didn't keep Judy on the phone long. "I'll call later in case Ashley needs to talk."

Chapter Fourteen

It was through her work with another unfortunate teenager that she happened to meet Detective Sam Warren, again. Actually the young man who was in trouble was his nephew, Tim. Janet had talked to Tim a couple of times at the high school and had hoped she was making progress.

Tim found out the hard way how dangerous it was to get involved with a gang. One of his friends has talked him into going with him to where the gang hung out. They got swept up in the crowd and found themselves in the middle of a street fight. Tim picked up a lead pipe he had found in an alley, but the others had knives. When confronted by someone much larger than himself, yielding a knife, he didn't have a chance. Lying on the pavement, he saw his friend and three others fall before he passed out. One of the lucky ones, Tim ended up in the hospital in serious condition. Sam came to the hospital as soon as he heard and sat with his sister, Annie, while Tim was in the operating room. His recovery was slow, but after three days he was able to leave the ICU to go to his own room.

It was about this time that Annie called Janet and asked

if she would talk to her son. The doctors had told Annie that his body would heal quickly, but it might take longer for the emotional scars to heal. Janet was standing outside Tim's hospital room talking to Annie when Sam walked up to them. Annie introduced Sam to Janet.

Sam offered her his hand in greeting. "Janet, it's nice to see you, again." Sam held on to her hand a little longer than necessary, wanting to prolong the moment.

A warm heat rose from his hand to flutter wildly in her belly. Not used to this type of reaction from just a handshake, she slipped her hand out of his grasp as soon as she could. "It's nice to see you again, Detective."

"Sam."

"Sam." Uncontrollably her eyes took in his ruggedly handsome features and tall muscular build. "I have to get back to the office." She pulled her eyes away from his to look at Annie. "I'll check my schedule once I get back to the office and then we can set up a few more sessions this week."

As Janet walked towards the elevators, Sam watched her shapely figure. He didn't realize his sister was talking to him until she shook his arm.

Surprised at his interest in Janet, Annie couldn't resist teasing him. "I haven't seen that look on your face in a long time. She's single, you know."

Sam smiled at her, lifting his eyebrows and grinning.

"Why is she here?"

"She counsels teens at the high school. Tim has talked with her twice before and made some progress. He likes her so I asked her to talk to him. She's a psychiatrist."

"Yes, we met before. She also helps the homeless."

Annie was happy for some distraction from her son's problems. "Interested?"

"Maybe, but no matchmaking. What happens happens." The doctor arrived and they both forgot about Janet for a while.

The next day, Sam walked in on a deep discussion between Janet and Tim. "Jake's been my friend since we were three. I trusted him. They tricked him, like they tricked me. We had no idea what we were walking into."

Unaware of their audience, Janet continued their discussion. "Jake paid a high price. Do you expect me to believe that the other guys didn't talk? Didn't they tell you some of what was going on?"

Tim didn't argue. "They made the gang sound cool."

While they talked, she sketched Tim and the room. In the background she sketched the street fight as she saw it, asking Tim questions. Her notes filled the margins.

Once Tim noticed his uncle standing by the door, all conversation stopped. Janet was not amused. "Don't you know how to knock?" The spell was broken. They wouldn't get any more done so she closed her drawing pad and prepared to leave.

Sam realized his mistake. Tim was staring out the window, not sure how much his uncle had heard. Janet touched her patient's arm, before leaving the room without saying a word to Sam.

He followed her out of the room grabbing her arm. "You don't have to leave."

"We're done for the day." Janet said, giving him an icy look until he released her arm.

"I'm family. My being there shouldn't bother you or Tim."

"You are still a police detective."

"That's my job."

"Next time, wait outside so I can do my job."

Sam watched her walk briskly down the hall towards the elevator. He should be sorry he upset her, but all he could do was smile. She was gorgeous when she was mad. Her eyes flashed fire. Sam wondered if that was the only time her eyes caught that spark. Their paths did not cross again for several months.

Chapter Fifteen

Detective Sam Warren was called to Riverside Park late one afternoon to the scene of a murder. This was the tenth homeless person to be murdered in a year. Pulling back the top of the tarp, he looked into the sad eyes and weathered face of a woman. She had been repeatedly stabbed and left on the park bench where she probably slept each night.

A few benches away, two women sat sobbing, their hands linked as they leaned towards each other for comfort. Sam walked over to them. "Are you the ones who found the body?"

"Gladys. Her name was Gladys." She sniffed trying to collect herself. "She had been sick for months, and was finally feeling better. We see her almost everyday. Gladys had agreed to come home with us tonight." The tears began to flow again. "Another day and she would have been off the streets."

"What's your name?"

"Sadie and this is my sister Elizabeth." She watched as he wrote down their names and address in his notebook.

They were interrupted by a uniformed officer. "Sir, we found this in her bag." Realizing he had been rude, the officer tipped his hat at the ladies. "Excuse the interruption."

Unfolding the heavy soiled white paper, Sam found an amazing likeness of the victim. It was dated almost a year before. "Did they find anything like this with the other bodies?" Sam asked the officer. He left to go find out.

Sadie leaned forward, already knowing what she would see. "Dr. Janet is quite talented, isn't she? She comes to the park almost every day to draw and share her lunch with our friends."

"Small world." Looking closer he saw her signature on the drawing.

"You know her?" Sadie asked.

He nodded, still studying the drawing. Looking up, he asked. "How do you know her?"

"I was a homeless person myself up until recently. Dr. Janet found my sister, and I went to live with her." Elizabeth squeezed Sadie's hand. "Gladys has been out on the streets a lot longer than I was." She swept her arms to the benches and the park around them.

"Do you know if she had any enemies?"

"Not Gladys. She was constantly giving things away to others. That's how she got so sick; she gave her blanket away to a mother for her children."

"Thank you, ladies." Sam patted Sadie's arm before

walking back to the other officers.

"Hey, Sam! You were right." The officer he had spoken to earlier ran up to him. "Every one of the victims had one of those drawings. What does it mean? Is that the killer's calling card?"

"No, it just means that Dr. Janet Leigh knew all of the victims. She helps the homeless." Giving the officer the drawing, he showed him the date. "I know her. I'll go talk to her."

A little later, Sam walked into Janet's outer office and was surprised to see her assistant was a man. Les checked the book even though he knew the last appointment of the day was in Janet's office. "Would you like to make an appointment, sir?"

Sam smiled and showed Les his badge. "I was hoping to see the doctor for a few minutes when she is free."

Les appraised the detective, holding onto his badge to check his name before releasing it. "You know the doctor?"

"Yes, we've met. She counsels my nephew, but this is police business."

Les was very protective of Janet. Now that he knew they were acquainted, he really checked Sam out. Thinking that this guy had possibilities, he thought Janet could use a hot affair with someone like him. He worried because she didn't date much.

Sam stood patiently while Les gave him the once over.

"What time do you think she will be able to see me?"

Les smiled warmly. "Won't be long now. This is her last appointment of the day. Would you like some coffee, tea, or a soda?"

"Coffee would be nice if you have some made. If not, I'll take a diet soda. Don't go to a lot of trouble."

"No trouble. I don't mind. I'll start the coffee and then tell her you are here." Les hummed a show tune as he moved about the tiny adjoining kitchen. Picking up the phone, he buzzed Janet in her office, keeping his voice low. "He's a hot one. Don't hurry with Mrs. Vincent. Make him wait a bit."

Janet had to hide a smile as she went back to her patient. Sometime later, Mrs. Vincent left her office. She loved to talk and Janet didn't rush her. In fact, Mrs. Vincent started talking to Sam as she left and it took him several minutes before he could break away to go into Janet's office. As he walked in, she had just finished her notes and was putting them in Mrs. Vincent's file.

Les followed Sam into the office saying he needed to get the files. Janet and Les both knew he could have waited until the next morning. Many days, Les was ready to leave shortly after the last appointment, running off to theatre practice or a class. Curiosity made him linger longer than usual. Not wanting to interfere if there was a chance for a relationship to bloom between Sam and Janet, he winked at Janet, took the files and left.

Sam sat in one of the chairs in front of her desk, sipping his coffee. Waiting until Les left, Janet sat back in her chair and smiled at Sam. Janet spoke first. "To what do I owe this visit?"

Her eyes twinkled as she smiled making him believe she was glad to see him again. He was reluctant to bring up the real reason he was here now that she was beginning to relax around him. "I was called to Riverside Park today to investigate another murder of a homeless person. Some creep likes to stab homeless people to death, this is the third one this month."

At the mention of Riverside Park, Janet's face grew pale. "I hadn't heard." She got up and walked to the window to stare out towards the park as if she could see it from her office.

"This is the part of my job that I don't like. Today's victim had one of your drawings in her bag. Sadie found her. I believe she is a friend of yours."

"Gladys." Janet said quietly before he could tell her.

"Yes." Slowly, he got up and stood behind her.

She was shaking her head. "I found her brother yesterday. Sadie and I had it all worked out. Gladys would go home with Sadie and Elizabeth. Tomorrow all of us were going to meet him for lunch. He was sure he could convince her to go home with him."

Sam saw her dab at her eyes. He pulled her against him,

Deadly Perception

resting his cheek against hers for a moment. "You can't save them all."

"I can try." She whispered.

Trying to change tactics, he brought up her drawing. "You are quite an artist. How did you ever get into psychiatry?"

"God gave me a gift and I wanted to use it to help people." She replied.

Sam wasn't sure he fully understood. "Could I see some more of your drawings?"

Moving away from him, she pulled her drawing pad from her briefcase. "Sure."

Taking the drawing pad, he sat back down. Flipping through the first few pages quickly, he slowed down as he saw the notes and small drawings that filled the margins. Sam thought about the reports he had heard on Janet from fellow officers about Janet helping others, and the first time he met her. He began to understand the true nature of her gift. Sam wanted to sit and go through every drawing slowly, but she was waiting for his response.

Laying the drawing pad on her desk, he went to her. Without a word, he folded her into his arms and held her. He kissed the top of her head and let her go.

She still thought he was too good to be true. "You don't think I'm crazy? Or weird?"

"No, why would I?" Sam teased her.

Surprised that she hadn't already scared him away, she

107

smiled, and then frowned. "What if I draw you and you don't like what I see?"

Walking back to her desk, he picked up the pad and a pencil and handed them to her. He went back to the chair in front of her desk and sat down, turning the chair to face her direction.

Amused that he had called her bluff, Janet turned to the next blank page, and let her fingers capture him on paper. His face was ruggedly handsome with broad cheekbones and a dimpled chin. Dark long lashes and thick brows framed the bluest eyes she had ever seen. His thick dark hair was a bit shaggy, but she decided she liked it that way. Earlier when he had touched her she had felt his warmth, his heat. As she drew him, she felt his desire for her, making her body tingle like tiny electric shocks touched her. The warmth grew until she felt the flames of desire taking her breath.

Sam sat and watched her draw. He liked watching the play of emotions in her face as she sketched. She would frown when concentrating and then the corners of her lips would lift in a soft smile like she liked what she saw.

His desire for her was different than that he felt for other women he had dated. It went deeper. Sam realized he needed to take it slow and easy with her. He didn't want just a tumble in the sheets with her, he wanted more.

Never had she felt this way about any man. The urgency she felt scared her. When her hands grew too clammy to hold the pencil, she gave up and handed him the drawing pad.

"Good. You really are good. There aren't any drawings or notes on the edges."

"No."

"Didn't you pick up on anything while you drew me?" Sam asked with a roguish smile.

"Sure, strong vibrations." As he stood up, she took his hand and put it on her chest over her heart so he could feel her reaction.

Sam took off his tie like it was cutting off his air. "You really should show your work." He tossed the drawing pad on top of her desk.

"Sam…?" This was a big step for her, this level of trust. "You feel it too?" Her words came out soft and breathless.

"Yes." He whispered huskily. As he touched her shoulders, he felt her body shaking. Looking into her eyes, he realized that it was as much from fear as it was desire.

"Are you afraid of me? I won't hurt you." It was important to him to understand the source of her fear. "I don't sleep around, if that is what is worrying you. I was married for a short time when I was young and foolish. Since then, I have only had a couple of relationships. Most women avoid more than a casual date with a police officer. Is there someone else?"

Shaking her head, she searched his face for any reaction as she spoke. "No one has ever wanted me. I scare people, or rather my gift of sight scares people away."

"I want you. I've wanted you ever since we met. Do you know you are even more beautiful when you are angry?"

"Sam, I take things very seriously."

"I'd like to be in a serious relationship with you." His statement surprised even him. Sam was amazed at the depth of his emotions when he was with her.

Putting her hands on his shoulders, she looked deep in his eyes. "Sam, I've never been with a man before."

Surprise filled his eyes briefly. When she touched her lips to his, they grew dark, dancing with the flame of desire. Kissing him was amazing; it was like another Janet was being brought to life.

Sam pulled away, giving her another wicked smile. "Chinese or Pizza?"

"Pizza, no anchovies." Janet laughed. "Do you want to eat here or go out?"

Sam thought about it before answering. "We can stay here."

"O.K., I'll call in the order, you get to answer the door." She crossed over to her desk. Dialing the number from memory, she placed their order. "20-30 minutes, that's not bad. Everyone else must be ordering Chinese."

Sam didn't say anything, just smiled. He was watching her as she walked across her office. Finally, he said, "Nice view from here."

Shaking her head as she smiled, she blushed and laughed. "I'm going to raid the refrigerator for sodas. What would you like?"

"Anything diet would be great."

"Be right back."

From the kitchen she pulled out placemats, napkins and utensils and set them out on the coffee table. They sat on the couch and sipped their sodas until the delivery person came. Over pizza they discussed their jobs, the parts they liked best and the parts that were unpleasant although necessary. Sam talked about his sister and her bad marriage. They talked about Tim, and how much better he was getting along. His relationship with Tim was getting stronger now that Tim was learning to trust him. He thanked Janet for that. What she had said that day in the hospital had made a lot sense. He wanted Tim to trust him in spite of his being a police detective. Janet told him about her dad and how lonely it was growing up.

Their eyes met as they talked and Janet felt his warmth, his sincerity, and his integrity. She admired him knowing he felt as strongly about his work as she felt about hers.

"I guess I should warn you." He began. "My schedule is terrible. I can get called at any time of day or night. It won't be easy, this new relationship of ours." Sam's eyes pleaded with her. He really wanted it to work.

At his words, her heart did a little giddy-up. "Well, I like challenges." She stopped to smile and touch his cheek.

"My schedule gets pretty crazy, too. I'm just starting a new project to help the city develop an old building on 78th into a homeless shelter. We can keep in touch by phone and make the time we have together count."

He kissed her. "I promise I will call as much as I can." Sam didn't want to make any promises that he couldn't keep.

They talked about her new project and a little about the murders he had been investigating. There were many facets of their work that they could not discuss with each other.

Glancing at his watch, Sam stood up and started gathering the remains of their supper. "I'll help you clean up and then I'll drive you home."

"I only live about three blocks from here."

"I know." He pulled her up beside him and kissed her. "It is part of my value-added service to make sure you get home safely."

She laughed and started straightening the office. Finding wood cleaner in the kitchen, she polished both her desk and the coffee table. Standing back to view her office, she made sure that everything was where it usually was.

Sam would have dropped her off at the front door of her building, but she insisted that he park his car and come up to her apartment. She showed him which parking place to use in the garage under the building, and introduced him to both the security guard and the doorman. Upstairs on the 10th floor she led him to apartment 1010 where she handed him her keys to open the door for her. She used a deadbolt as well as the regular lock.

He showed appreciation for the security the building offered. Following her into the apartment, Sam set her keys on the table by the door. Janet turned on the closest lamp. "I should get home." Taking a business card out of his wallet, he wrote his home phone and cell phone numbers on the back.

"Good Night." Sam kissed her lightly. "We'll talk tomorrow."

"Good Night, Sam." Janet closed the door and leaned against it smiling.

In the morning, Janet poured a cup of coffee and sat down to read the newspaper. She was having a simple breakfast, cereal and coffee. Gladys' murder covered the front page, although her name had been withheld. Janet read the story sadly, trying to keep eating although her appetite was fading.

Suddenly she remembered Gladys' brother and their scheduled meeting that day. Janet picked up Sam's card and dialed his home phone number first. When there was no answer, she tried his office.

"Sam." He answered in a clipped tone.

Janet was wary. "Sam, this is Janet."

Immediately his tone changed. "Good morning!"

"Sorry for calling so early, but I just remembered Gladys' brother. Has anyone called him?"

"I don't think anyone has figured out who her next of kin is and I haven't spoken to anyone yet this morning. You were supposed to meet him today, right? Why don't you call him? Wait. Let me see if I can get this conference call thing to work on my phone. Be patient with me. I may have to get Sue to help me get this thing to work. What's his number?"

Janet read the phone number, and then held the line while Sam tried to connect them all in a conference call.

"Janet. I have Jake Nichols on the line." Sam invited her to speak first.

"Jake, I'm sorry for calling you so early." Janet greeted him.

"Good morning, Janet." Jake replied.

"Jake, Sam and I are calling with some bad news. There's no easy way to tell you this, but Gladys was murdered in the park late yesterday." Janet tried to be gentle.

"The woman in the newspaper? That was Gladys?" Jake asked in disbelief.

"I'm afraid so." Janet felt bad for him.

"Jake, we need you to come down and identify the body. It's just a formality as a friend of hers already identified her at the scene." Sam told Jake the address.

Janet wanted to help him. "Jake, please let me know if there is anything I can do."

114

"Thanks, Janet. You've been a good friend. I should be thanking you. I want to take her back home to Ohio where our parents are buried. Thank you, Sam. I'll be down there in about an hour."

Jake hung up and so did Sam.

Janet threw out her uneaten cereal and cold coffee. She decided to go into work and make some phone calls.

By the time Les arrived she was going over her notes on the morning patients. She found the files on Les' desk. Les was not a morning person so he always went into the small kitchen and made a pot of coffee the minute he arrived. By habit, he did not show his face in the office until he had at least one cup. Once the caffeine kicked in he usually brought her a cup and greeted her.

"Good Morning!" This morning he made himself comfortable in the chair on the other side of her desk, and sipped his coffee. Smiling mischievously, he was impatient to hear about her evening. "Come on. Tell all. What's he like?"

"Who?" She didn't know if she wanted to discuss her new love life with anyone. It was too special. But, Les was her best friend.

"Don't tell me you let him just leave here after I left last night?" Les looked disappointed.

Shaking her head, she got serious. "Gladys was the latest stabbing victim in the park. Sam came to tell me. One more

115

day and we would have gotten her off the streets."

"I'm sorry." Les knew she really liked Gladys. He sat quietly, sipping his coffee.

Finally, he started to leave, but she stopped him with her words. "By the way, Sam is wonderful, exciting and very hot."

Wide eyed, Les looked at her more closely and could see the changes. She had a glow about her and her eyes smiled even when her mouth was serious. "Did you two, you know?"

"No. We just kissed." Unable to keep a straight face any longer, she started grinning and laughing. "I hope this works out Les. I really like him."

"I'm so happy for you! He really is good looking. Tell me more."

"Les!" Janet's face turned pink. "We are good together, we fit."

"Does he know about your gift? Your second sight?"

Janet looked at him closely to judge how he saw her gift. "Yes and he's O.K. with it. You and I have never discussed my gift before."

He shrugged. "I see your notes, and I've watched you over the years. You seemed a little sensitive about the privacy of your notes, but I was curious. It is unusual when a doctor does not want her notes transcribed." She didn't seem upset with him or with what he had just confessed. "So, Sam was O.K. with it?"

"Didn't seem to bother him at all."

"Good." Les came around the desk and gave her a hug. "I am so happy for you."

Janet gave him a twinkling smile. "Thank you."

They both heard someone come in out front, which was their signal to get to work.

Chapter Sixteen

Sam called her at least once a day. If she wasn't at the office and he had free time, he would ask Les where she was and surprise her. Janet had a cell phone, but as he soon found out, turned it off when she was with patients. He would show up at the park at lunch time, or be waiting for her when she got out of whatever meeting or appointment she had that day. They would sit and talk or go to a café to take advantage of what time they had together.

Saturday night became their date night. Sam took her to his favorite Italian restaurant. That first Saturday, Janet was wearing a new black dress with large scarf as a shawl and a beaded bag. Sam had whistled when he saw how the dress showed off her long legs and nice figure. He made her turn around to show off for him. "You look great! We had better go now, or we might not make it to the restaurant."

Janet smiled with delight as he took her arm and helped her into his dark blue sedan. She wanted to look special for him and had never spent that much time getting ready before.

Sam was dressed in a charcoal gray suit, something he normally would never wear to the office. When he went into work for a few hours the other officers had teased him, but he didn't mind. He knew they were happy for him.

Being their first real date out together, they were each a little nervous. A comfortable silence settled between them during the short drive to the restaurant. Sam took one of the parking places out back where the sign said reserved parking. They went in the back door into the kitchen. A large man dressed in white from head to toe with a floppy chef's hat greeted them warmly. "Sam! You haven't been here in a while. I would be mad at you, but you brought a beautiful lady to see us." Wiping his hands on his apron, he came to meet them.

"Hey, George!" The two men made a big deal hugging each other and clapping each other on the back. "This is Dr. Janet Leigh." Sam stood back to see Janet's reaction to his friend.

George took her hand and kissed it, then pulled her into his arms for a bone-crushing hug. "You must be special if Sam brought you here. He's never brought anyone else here except for Annie and Tim of course."

"It's nice to meet you, George." Janet said smiling and laughing at how friendly he was. About fifty, he was tall and broad, like he ate a lot of his own cooking. She immediately liked him.

"You leave everything to me. No need to order. I will serve you a meal fit for a queen." George led the way out of the kitchen into the busy dining room and motioned for the maitre d'. "Tony, Sam brought his lovely lady to visit us tonight. Show them to my table and take special care of them."

"Thank you." Janet smiled at George as he went back into the kitchen. Tony led them to a table in a corner alcove that Sam had never noticed before. It was very private, very cozy. Janet slid into the curved bench and Sam slid in next to her. Tony moved the table closer once they were seated.

Sam thanked him. Janet watched Tony walk away and looked at Sam in amazement. Before she could say a word, a waiter was there to pour ice water with lemon. Another waiter set the table and lit a candle. As soon as he left, the first one reappeared with a bottle of Merlot and two beautiful crystal glasses. Sam tasted the wine and nodded for the waiter to go ahead and pour.

Finally they were left alone for a few moments to sit back and enjoy the wine. Sam was ready to confess that he hadn't planned any of this. "I think George really likes you."

"He wants this to be special for us." Janet clicked her glass against his. "To us."

"To us." They each took a sip of wine without taking their eyes off of each other. Slowly they lowered their glasses to the table and tasted each other. It was several moments before they returned to their wine.

A waiter brought salads and garlic bread. He offered them fresh ground parmesan and pepper. They ate slowly, enjoying the food and the atmosphere. When she had finished the last bite of salad, a waiter appeared to take away the dishes and bring clean plates. It took both waiters to bring their main course. There were generous portions of several seafood and pasta dishes for them to share. They each took helpings of their favorites. Sam offered her a bite of his seafood Alfredo, and she gave him a bite of her ravioli. They tried at least a bite or two of everything, but there was way too much food for two people.

When they could eat no more, the waiter took the plates away. Another brought coffee. Sam only had a chance to drink one sip of his coffee when his cell phone rang. "Sorry." He took the call. "I have to go. I'm sorry. I'll get you a cab." He looked at her with regret in his eyes.

"I'm going with you."

"You sure?" He didn't take time to argue.

"Let's go." She followed him out.

"Tony, put it on my account, O.K." Sam asked as they moved through the restaurant.

George didn't seem surprised to see them as they came through the kitchen. He handed Janet a bag with two foam boxes inside and kissed her on the cheek. "Come see us again soon."

She barely had a chance to thank George as Sam pulled her out the door. Janet had to admit that it was exciting, going fast with the red blinking light on top the car. Sam was a careful driver and took no chances even though he needed to hurry. Instinctively she picked up her drawing pad that she had left in the car and found a pencil in her purse.

Pulling over, Sam parked behind two other police cars. Boarded up and covered with graffiti, the old building was near Riverside Park. It should have been demolished many years ago. "You'd better wait here." Sam was worried about leaving her alone, but wasn't sure it would be any safer inside.

Watching Sam run up the stairs and into the building, Janet opened her door and swung her feet outside so she faced the building. Flipping open her drawing pad, she started sketching the building towards the top of the page. It was only a few moments before her hand seemed to have a mind of its own.

"Monroe." Tears stung her eyes as she wrote his name below his likeness. There was more, she could pick up on more. Her feet carried her slowly up the steps to the second floor where several officers stood outside in the hall. None of them tried to stop her as she stood outside the apartment watching Sam work for a few minutes. One of them recognized her when he saw the drawing pad she carried and went to tell Sam she was waiting.

"Janet?" He was worried about her being there.

Showing him the drawing, she gave him a worried look. Flipping to a new page, she brushed past him into the apartment. Walking slowly around the room without stepping on anything that littered the floor, she continued to draw. She stopped and closed her eyes. Turning around slowly, her eyes remained closed until she made a full circle. Opening her eyes, she started sketching and filled five pages in a short time.

Another officer came up the stairs as they all stood watching and was immediately shushed before he could speak.

When she came out of the apartment, Janet let Sam lead her back down the hall where they could talk. "What happened in there?"

"The energy was so strong. I could feel Monroe's emotions as he was attacked. There was something more, the killer I think. I couldn't get much on him, but it felt like he was there in the room watching me. It was amazing how strong the energy was. I've never experienced anything like that before."

"Do you think the killer is nearby?" Sam asked.

"I'm sure of it."

Sam sent some of his officers to search the building and the area around it. He called dispatch and asked for more cars to search the area. Chris was coming up the stairs.

"Janet is sure that he is here somewhere close by watching us." They talked about the crime scene. "Let's go look at Janet's drawings. Maybe she has picked up on something we've missed."

Janet smiled at him. He never questioned the validity of her drawings, and seemed to accept her help with the case without reservation. They stood at the doorway to the apartment comparing what they could see from the door to what was in her drawings.

"You've sketched him before in the park?" Sam asked.

She nodded. "Twice."

"Did you give him a drawing?"

"Yes." Janet replied. "This first drawing shows how happy he was that day. I did this one in the car, before I came upstairs. I knew it was Monroe."

"Look at these marks on his cheek. Whoever did this smacked the old man and his hand left a print. I didn't see it when I looked at the body." Sam pointed out details on the second drawing.

"The mark may not show on his face, I draw what I see." Janet explained.

Sam was excited in a way Janet had never seen. He examined her drawings for every detail like he did the crime scene. "We found the knife, same type as before, a generic kitchen type knife. What's this? I didn't see any footprints. All of us were tromping around in there, but maybe we can

124

still get something." Sam hoped.

Chris asked an officer standing nearby. "Get someone to bring a light up here and try to keep everyone else out of there. We need to check for footprints. Janet's drawing shows footprints all around the body. They could be the killers, Monroe's, or one of ours, but we need to check it out."

"Nothing on the jerk that did this?" Chris asked.

"No, sorry." Shaking her head, Janet tore out the drawings and gave them to Sam. Chris took the one that showed the footprints and directed the other officer who was in control of the light.

While she watched them, she drew the crime scene. She was restless and felt like she should be doing something. The coroner arrived and was anxious to get the body moved.

She continued to draw while they all worked the crime scene. Sam and Chris were doing what they did best. They had basically forgotten about her, but she found watching them fascinating. When Sam was finally ready to go, she handed him the drawing pad as a place to store the other drawings. He would not find the other drawings that filled the drawing pad until much later when he returned to his office.

Sam stopped by in the morning. Janet had made coffee and was sitting at the table reading the Sunday newspaper. He brought bagels and cream cheese.

Together, they poured over the newspaper as they ate. The murder dominated the front page, along with the many unsolved cases of the past year. The newspaper nicknamed the killer "Homeless Harry." Janet could see where this nickname might actually make the killer angrier with the homeless. "I hope all of this publicity does not increase the frequency of the murders. Whoever the killer is, this publicity could only increase his resentment against the homeless."

Sam looked over at her, knowing she could be right. "Or make him kill more often if he likes the publicity."

"I don't think this guy likes publicity, but I think he reads and listens to what they say about him. He may do something just to prove that the press is wrong about him."

He appreciated her viewpoint. "The FBI is coming today to help in the investigation. I'm going to suggest that we need you as a consultant on this case."

Janet hated the thought of any publicity about her gift of sight, but he was right, she was too close to the case to back out now. The visions would keep coming whether she liked it or not.

"Why don't you go in with me when I show them your drawings so you can answer any questions? At least we will get to spend a little time together."

Janet went with Sam, but as it turned out, the FBI was not interested in Janet's drawings at all. They saw no value in her help. Sam assured her that they would change their minds later. Temporarily relieved, Janet spent the rest of the day working on her homeless shelter project, calling builders at home and trying to solicit their free services. It was difficult to catch these men during the week, and she was hoping that they may feel more charitable on Sunday.

With the FBI underfoot throughout their investigation, Sam was even busier. He tried to call her every day, but missed a few. When he did call, he usually missed her and talked to Les to make sure she was O.K.

On Friday, he left a message. "Tell her that I will meet her at our restaurant Saturday night. With the FBI watching everything we do, I'm lucky if I get to do more than fall asleep at my desk for an hour or so. Thanks!" Sam hung up a few minutes before Janet came back into the office.

Les gave her the message, and heard her mumble, "He better be there." She missed him. It was frustrating not being able to talk to him even when she knew he had very good reasons for not calling her. "Patience, I need to be patient." She reminded herself.

Les smiled at her. "Speaking of patients."

She laughed and smiled at him. "O.K. funny boy. Show the next patient in."

"Funny Boy. Hmm. That would be a great name for my next play." Les gave her a grin and winked at her.

She was still smiling when the patient came into her

office.

Janet became a regular fixture in George's kitchen. If Sam was late, she would often put on an apron and find something to do to help. She found it relaxing and enjoyed everyone who worked there. They joked around a lot, but also took their work seriously. After several Saturdays with her helping them, they began saving jobs for her, things that she would enjoy like arranging trays or decorating desserts. The restaurant did a lot of parties and catering.

Sam always showed up, but rarely on time. One time he got there when George was helping her into a cab. It was George who scolded him for arriving so late. Janet took the cab home alone, smiling. She knew it would be at least a half hour before he showed up at her door. George insisted that Sam stop at a florist on his way, and made him promise to never do it again without calling. "Do you want to lose her?"

One thing that gave Sam some satisfaction during this time was that the FBI had not been able to find any more clues to solve the murders than his own men. He really wanted to solve the murders, but there always had been some competition between the federal and local police anytime they were working the same cases.

Not happy with the progress on the case, Sam enlisted Janet's help. "I thought of something you can do that would help this case. I don't know why we didn't think of it before.

Instead of seeking out the homeless in the park each day, I want you to look for people who seem out of place in the park. Someone who is watching the homeless like you are or just looks suspicious. After all these months, we don't have any leads. Maybe if we check out these people we will run into the murderer. It is a long shot, but we don't have anything else to go on right now. All we know is that this guy hates the homeless and he stabs all his victims with cheap common kitchen knives."

Janet wasn't sure it would help with his case, but she agreed to try it. Flipping through her drawing pad, she found two that might fit his description. They didn't seem to be enjoying the park like everyone else.

She promised to call if she saw any others. Sam, Chris, or another officer would stop by and get the drawings. They kept this up for two weeks. It was getting colder and not as many people came to the park. This made some people stand out from the others. For their efforts, they busted two parole violators and a man with a lot of unpaid parking tickets.

Janet came to the conclusion that the killer would not fit the profile of the people who normally hung out at the park each day, and she did not think that the killer would be obvious about observing the homeless if he did so. Most of the murders were committed late in the day or under the cover of darkness. However, she did believe that the killer chose each victim ahead of time, which meant the killer saw the victim on a previous occasion or followed the victim to know where they liked to hang out at night. Her instincts told her the victims were not chosen randomly. There had to be some connection between the killer and the victim.

Speculating seemed silly, but Janet found herself imagining under what circumstances the killer might run into the homeless on a regular basis. Maybe he passed them on the way to the subway station, or in the alley behind where the killer worked. No, she didn't think that fit the victims she knew. Most of the victims she knew went to one of the missions or food kitchens at least once or twice a week, if not once a day for a hot meal, but otherwise hung out in or near the park.

Going with the assumption that this could be the connection, Janet toured each of the establishments set up for the homeless over the course of a week. She called it homework for planning the facility she was working on. There was one shelter, the closest one to Riverside Park, which served meals late in the day. She saw a lot of familiar faces there.

That night she told Sam what she had found and her theory. With no better leads to go on, Sam decided to put one of his own guys there undercover as one of the homeless. Meanwhile, they would run background checks on every social worker and volunteer that worked there.

Construction on her homeless shelter was going well.

The inside of the old building had been in bad shape, but the structure itself was solid. Since the weather grew colder, she appealed to her volunteer workers to hurry the project along. She hoped to open it by Christmas.

Once she had made a list of the things that needed to be purchased, she started contacting various companies to get the best price quotes. She gave every supplier the same spiel about supporting a good cause with donations. But after all the donations were deducted, she still needed $10,000 for furniture, equipment, supplies, and start up expenses.

One of Janet's clients, Frannie Sullivan, was the social event manager at the Hilton. It took very little to persuade her to help put together a benefit party. Frannie even talked the Hilton into offering a banquet room free of charge. Les volunteered to do the invitations. Frannie talked to several florists who offered flower arrangements for the occasion. Restaurants around the city offered to supply hors d'oeuvres. They decided to do a cash bar. Invitations went out to all the businesses and all the socialites in town. Because many of these people left the city on weekends, Thursday night was chosen for the big event. Tickets to the event sold fast so they printed more. A larger room had to be found for the event.

A few days before the big event, the newspaper sent a reporter to interview Janet. They asked about her personal life and she suddenly was not sure if Sam would want everyone to know about their relationship. Excusing herself, she went to another room to call him.

"Sure you can tell them. I'm in this relationship 100%. You can tell the whole world if you want."

Her heart did a little skip in excitement. "Me, too. See you later."

"Got to go. Bye." Sam hung up.

She stared at the phone for a few minutes and found herself grinning.

Returning to the reporter, she composed herself. "My boyfriend works for the local police department as a detective. That's why I needed to check with him first." She told the reporter she had met Sam when his nephew, one of her patients, wound up in the hospital. It was not really the first time they had met, but it kept the homeless murders out of the conversation.

Later that day Sam turned around in the police station and was quickly blinded by a camera flash. The same reporter had come out of curiosity to see Sam. She asked him if he would be escorting Janet to the benefit. "Yes. I'm very proud of Janet's hard work on this project. It will be very successful. I'm sure of it. Will you be there?" Sam asked in return.

"Wouldn't miss it. Thanks!" The reporter left as quickly as she came.

Chapter Seventeen

Thursday came and other than a few phone calls, Janet's day was fairly routine. She did leave work early to get ready. Worried about the little details, she wanted to get there early. Sam was at her apartment when she arrived, already dressed. "I knew you would want to get there early. Frannie made us an early reservation in the dining room so we can get a bite to eat before it all starts. That way you will be close by if something comes up that you need to handle."

"I'm too nervous to eat."

"You have to eat. Les said you wouldn't stop for lunch today."

Looking at him in amazement, she just couldn't argue. "I am so lucky to have you."

Sam stopped trying to fix his bowtie. "Better get dressed, Cinderella."

What Sam did not tell her was how concerned the department was about another murder being committed that night. Every available officer was assigned to patrol the Riverside Park area. There was also some concern about someone sabotaging the event. He was not the only officer who would be attending the benefit. Janet had been so successful at promoting the event that it became a huge concern.

One front page newspaper story published that morning talked about both the benefit and the homeless murders. Everyone was hoping the killer did not read the papers. After the radio and television stations picked up the same theme, it would have been very difficult to miss the publicity.

Janet mingled with the crowd and was quite pleased with the turnout. Tables had been set up at the back of the room for a silent auction of items donated by businesses in the area. At a mid-point in the evening they were going to auction off some of the larger donations. Already she had received more than her original $10,000 goal from people who pressed checks into her hands as she walked about the room.

With no pockets and worried about holding so much money, she kept handing the checks to Sam. She hoped his pockets would be bulging by the end of the evening. Janet had no idea the benefit would raise so much money. A foundation would have to be set up to distribute the rest of the funds. Her head was spinning with all the excitement.

Sam was never very far away, which was very comforting. One time he received a call and had to leave the room. She found Chris standing at her elbow within minutes. Her normal instincts kicked in and she immediately realized what an event like this could mean to their murder investigation. Feeling selfish and slightly stupid, she touched his elbow and leaned close. "Has anything happened?"

Forgetting how astute she was, he was momentarily surprised. "No, all calm so far. We do have some homeless people who have started to gather out in front of the hotel. They heard about the event and thought they were invited. Sam went to see the manager, who is naturally upset."

Janet saw Frannie nearby and walked towards her. "Is the other banquet room still open?"

"Yes, I think so. Why?"

Janet told Frannie what Chris just told her. "Does the kitchen have a lot of leftover food? Please see if you can arrange for food to be served to the homeless outside. Tell them to send me the bill. We've raised so much money tonight, and I don't want them to go away hungry."

Frannie went to see what she could do.

"Chris, go catch Sam and tell him. Don't let them send the people away, please?"

Not wanting to leave her alone, he called to the other officers in the room to stay with Janet. Maggie showed up at Janet's side and introduced herself.

Management was not happy with the idea, but realized the publicity would be good for the hotel. Sam and Chris were surprised to see 40-50 people waiting, blocking the entrance. They were allowed to enter the hotel. Bellhops helped the police officers direct their homeless visitors through the lobby quietly and into the banquet room. There was an emergency exit off of that room that they could use when they were ready to leave.

In the kitchen, the refrigerators were turned inside out for anything that could be quickly heated and served. Bread, fruit, cheese, and crackers were set out immediately, along with urns of coffee. A couple of late diners in the restaurant heard the commotion and asked what was happening and volunteered to help the skeleton crew that was left in the restaurant.

As the last person entered the hotel, Sam noticed a man sitting on the sidewalk with his back to the building. As they moved closer, Chris pointed out the puddle of blood spreading across the sidewalk. He called for an ambulance, but they could not find a pulse. About 50, the man was dressed in a ragged wool coat. They could see the surprise still in his eyes from when he was stabbed.

Photos were taken and the other homeless were questioned, but no one seemed to notice the poor man being murdered. One man did say he saw a young man in a blue parka and stocking cap walk by and push a few of them. A wide search of the area was made, but no one was found that fit the description. The body was quietly taken away so no one at the benefit would panic.

Sam and Chris found Janet sitting alone at a table with Maggie standing close by. Looking very sad, she looked up at them. "His name was Sam, too. He liked to wash cars, and worked at one of the gas stations when he wasn't too drunk to work. The manager of the station made him shower and put on overalls before work each day. He made sure he ate a good lunch, and sometimes fed him breakfast or supper. Sam had a cot in the locker room where he was allowed to stay at night, but he still slept on the street most nights. Last time I saw Sam, he said he hadn't had a drop to drink in a week. There was hope for him."

"Did you say anything to anyone?"

Janet shook her head. Glancing at her watch, she took a deep breath and got up. "It's time for the auction. That will keep everyone busy for a while."

She headed for the stage where the auctioneer was standing near by. Janet got up on the stage to introduce him. The crowd began clapping before she could speak. Such an overwhelming response surprised her. Motioning them to stop, she started speaking several times before they quieted down. "Thank you, everyone. We have some great people in this room. I am overwhelmed at your generosity, but I hope that your pockets are not quite empty." She paused as some of the crowd laughed. "We have some great items for sale tonight. I hope you will be equally generous with your bids. Now, let me introduce our auctioneer, one of Sotheby's retired auctioneers, Greg Allen." As the crowd clapped, Janet stepped back and let the auctioneer and his helpers do what they were good at.

Bidding for the items went high. The first item, an art print that she knew sold in the art museum gift shop for about $350 sold for $5,000. Confident that the sale was off to a good start, she worked the crowd. An up and coming interior designer had offered her services to redecorate a room and was quite please to see her gift certificate go for $50,000. This event would bring her a lot of new business. Many smart businessmen and women donated merchandise and services for the event in the hope that the publicity would increase their customer list to include the elite of the city attending that night.

By the time the partygoers were ready to leave, all signs of the murder and the homeless had been discreetly removed. The hotel manager stood by the door and said good night to the guests as they left. Bellhops and doormen helped them enter waiting limousines and taxis.

Sam and Chris sat with Janet and Fannie as the cash and checks were collected into one large envelope. Frannie put the envelope in the hotel safe until an armed guard would come to pick it up in the morning to take it to the bank. Two uniformed police officers would stay at the hotel in the lobby for the rest of the night as a precaution.

Janet had already set up a checking account, but would

have to set up savings and investment accounts. Now that so much money was involved, she was worried about accounting for every penny. She planned on being there when the envelope was opened and would count it herself to verify the bank's figures. Copies would be made of all checks so a donor list could be developed, and a large ad would be placed in the newspaper to thank everyone.

Sam dropped her off at home. After only a few hours of restless sleep, Janet read the newspaper while eating breakfast. The benefit filled several pages in the main section of the paper as well as the society pages. A separate article told about the impromptu dinner that was put together for the homeless. The front page was filled with the story of the latest murder. Only one photographer had snapped a shot in front of the hotel, and that was not until the coroner came to take the poor man away. Janet was surprised to find one of her drawings on the front page to show what the murdered Sam looked like. Janet was glad the drawing was small so no one could read her signature.

Most of the TV channels and radio stations were talking about her benefit and the homeless murders. They were linked together in almost every story and her name was mentioned. Les had to deal with a lot of phone calls and she had to take a cab to the bank to try to avoid the reporters. They were there waiting for her when she came out.

She issued one statement thanking all the people who

attended the benefit for their generosity, but refused to comment on the murders.

A few days later a fire erupted in one of the subway tunnels. Five homeless people died, and two more were seriously injured. The homeless that died were blamed for starting the fire to keep warm. News stories came out about helping the homeless get off the streets, and Janet's work with the homeless again became big news.

Chapter Eighteen

Saturday night, Janet met Sam at the restaurant. She sat in the kitchen while she waited, talking to George and his associates. He was trying out a new recipe.

"Did I ever tell you about Sam as a little boy?" George entertained her as he cooked. "Sam has always liked Italian food. As a boy, his grandma fixed special meals for him every Sunday. My mama was a long time friend of Sam's grandma and after she died I was always invited to Sunday dinner. I showed up early and volunteered to help. She taught me how to cook. So as a young man, I was determined to become a great chef and open my own restaurant. Taste this. Is there too much garlic?"

Janet took the offered spoon and tasted the sauce. "It's pretty hard to use too much garlic. It's good."

"But? It needs something, right?"

"How about a touch of cumin?" She offered.

George gave her a thoughtful look and went back to his sauce.

"So how long have you had this restaurant?" She asked,

141

hoping he would continue his story.

With his back bent over the stove, George went on with his story. "It turned out that Sam's grandma was a miserly old lady who had put away a large nest egg for Sam. When she died, Sam was surprised to find out she had saved over $150,000. She had lived very simply all her life. So simply that there was very little to get rid of when Sam went through her effects. She owned only a few dresses, a pair of slippers, and two pair of shoes. Sam was sad to think she gave up so much just to for him, but I think that she was quite happy living that way."

"Sam found this building. It was one the city wanted to renovate and they were willing to sell it for back taxes. He bought it, dragged me down here and told me to get to work. We worked every free moment on this place fixing it up. It took six long months to get the restaurant open. After that Sam left it all up to me. He wanted to be my silent partner. I owe him so much, but he is happy with the check I send him every month."

As he stirred the sauce, the kitchen grew quiet. She realized that everyone was waiting to see what George would think of the sauce. "Amazing!" He said as he tried a small spoonful. "Just what it needed."

Taking a small dish of pasta that his assistant handed him, he spooned some of the sauce over it. He took a fork and handed one to Janet. They each tried a bite. "It is good."

She smiled, happy to be included in George's experiment.

Sam entered the kitchen at that moment. George handed the plate to his assistant and went to greet him. "Sam, I was about to ask Janet to marry me. That way she could come work for me."

"Sorry, George. She's already taken." Sam put his arm around her shoulders.

"I bet I know how to change her mind." George looked at Sam to see if he had any objections and found his friend smiling. "Janet, come with me. I want to show you my place."

He led them to a door down a back hall in the restaurant, and up a staircase to the top floor. As they walked up the three flights of stairs he pointed to other apartments that they rented out. Unlocking the door at the top of the stairs, he opened the door and flipped on the light.

Rich dark wood furniture filled the loft apartment, most of it antique. "This is beautiful! She explored the room looking at his collection of vases and artwork. "Where did you ever find all of these things?"

"Some were from the family, but many pieces I picked up at flea markets, auctions, and garage sales. I love to go to sales and find new shops to explore."

Janet fell in love with a blue and white vase with a fluted top. "You must go to different sales than I do. You have a charming apartment."

"Thank you, but you haven't seen the best part." George led her to a sliding glass door off of the kitchen. He flipped a switch and watched her face as she took in the lush greenery and colorful flowers of his rooftop garden. In the center of the garden was an arbor covered with roses, which shaded a carved wooden bench. Flower boxes sat on the edges of the rooftop with vines spilling over the sides.

Excitement bubbled inside her as she came back to them. Standing on tiptoe, she brushed George's cheek with a kiss. "It is absolutely lovely. I've never seen anything like it anywhere. How do you possibly find the time to do all of this?"

Janet walked around the garden again, and then came back to them full of smiles. "Thank you for sharing this with me, George."

"Sam, you'd better hang on to her. I might steal her from you." George patted her cheek.

Taking Sam's arm she followed them back inside and down the stairs. George signaled to Tony and he showed them to their table.

Janet kissed Sam after he sat down beside her in their favorite booth. "Hi! How was your day?"

"Better since I got here. How's the shelter work coming?"

"Good. Almost on schedule." They shared a smile.

Picking up her drawing pad and a pencil she began

to sketch. She stopped at intervals to sip her wine. Sam watched a likeness of George come to life on the page with his rooftop garden in the background. She spent a lot of time on the sketch, shading and adding more detail until she thought it was just right. Sam was amazed at her talent.

When the waiter brought their meal, Janet asked him to ask George to come out when he had time. They ate in companionable silence, letting the good company and cozy atmosphere erase the stress from their busy day. Both of them looked forward to these dinners every week.

George brought out desert even though Janet had asked him to stop bringing her fattening delicacies after the huge meals he served them. When she gave him one of the looks that he had grown to love, he laughed. "I just brought one for you to share."

Janet shook her head and smiled. "I have something for you." Tearing out the drawing carefully, she handed it to him.

He loved the drawing, especially the garden. "Thank you. You did this without looking at the garden or me again? The detail is amazing." He kissed her cheek. I'm going to have it framed." Not waiting for her answer, George ran off with the drawing, showing it to his customers as he passed on his way to the kitchen.

Sam shook his head in amazement. He had never seen his friend so overwhelmed by emotion. "George will do anything you ask of him. You have totally charmed him. I've never seen him like this."

She just smiled as she took a bite of the luscious desert.

Chapter Nineteen

Waking with a start, Janet sat up in bed early Monday morning gasping for air. She grabbed the phone and dialed Sam's home number.

"She's gasping for air. He punctured her lung when he stabbed her." Janet said before he could say hello.

"Where is she?"

"In the park." She brushed the hair out of her eyes when there was none. "He found her in a drainage pipe, in some bushes left by some workmen last time they fixed that stretch of road. It has become her home, a dry cozy place to sleep, her hideaway."

He could not see Janet's face, which reflected the victim's pain and fear at being attacked in what had become her refuge. "How could he violate her like that? Sam, he left her like that to die. You've got to find her." Janet was sobbing. Realizing they were wasting time, she jumped up and started grabbing for warm clothes.

"I'll pick you up." Sam dialed Chris' number while trying to put on his pants. "Meet me at the Riverside Park with backup and an ambulance. She's in a sewer pipe near a road in the park hidden by some bushes. That's all I know. I'll call you back after I pickup Janet."

"Janey, we need better directions." He said as she got in the car.

Sam barely had time to stop the car before Janet jumped out. "Jenna!" Janet called out as she ran straight for the bushes she had described with the other officers close behind. "Hold on Jenna! Where are the medics? Please tell me they are here?" She yelled over her shoulder as she ran. The pipe was narrower than they had expected. Entirely hidden, they would never have found it in time if Janet hadn't led them to it.

Using his radio, Chris called the paramedics with directions. In moments the ambulance stopped on the road and rushed to their side. Sam moved back. Janet kept talking to her. "Jenna! Hold on. Help is here." Janet talked to her continuously as the paramedics frantically worked to save her life.

One well-meaning officer tried to pull Janet out of the way. Jenna's vital signs dropped quickly. The closest medic pulled Janet back to hold Jenna's hand. Her touch and her voice seemed to make a difference. They needed that edge. After receiving a pointed look from the paramedic and Sam, the officer stepped back out of the way.

"Jenna! I'm here, honey. We need you, Jenna! Just hold

on." With Janet's help, the medics were able to stabilize Jenna enough to move her to the waiting ambulance. Janet held her hand all the way to the hospital.

In the emergency room, again Janet was physically pushed from Jenna's side. "Hey! You let the Doc hold the young lady's hand. It's the only life line she has right now." The paramedic said as he gently pushed Janet back towards Jenna. No one else argued about her being there.

"What kind of doctor are you?" The attending physician asked her as he worked on Jenna.

"A psychiatrist. My name is Janet Leigh."

He made no comment, but raised his eyebrows in surprise. "You know her?"

"We met twice in the park. She's very shy, but she seemed to trust me." Janet looked down in surprise as Jenna squeezed her hand weakly. "Oh, Jenna! Hang on to me sweetie. These people are here to help you."

Her eyes opened once, then closed as the bright lights hurt her eyes.

"Hey! Jenna! Nice meeting you. I'm your doctor, Sal. We're going to fix it so you can breathe easier."

She responded to his deep masculine voice like she did Janet's. Jenna opened her eyes and looked into the handsomest face she had ever seen and smiled. Laughing with joy, Janet gladly let Sal work his magic.

Sal smiled and laughed, but he didn't miss a beat talking

to Jenna. "You can breathe a little better now, right?"

Jenna nodded.

"We're going to take you up to the operating room."

Jenna raised her hand towards Sal with a question in her eyes.

"Will I operate? You bet. It would be my pleasure. How about if Janet comes up with us and keeps you company while I scrub up?"

Jenna's eyes were bright when she nodded. Janet took her hand again and stayed close by while they moved her, continuing to hold her hand until it was time to operate.

Catching a glimpse of her appearance in the window, Janet decided to use the time wisely and go home, shower and change her clothes. The officer she met at her fundraiser, Maggie Henderson, had been assigned to stay with Jenna and interview her as soon as possible. Maggie had a lot of experience with runaway teenagers. Jenna was no longer a teenager, but Maggie had volunteered to come to the hospital. Janet talked to Maggie briefly before leaving, promising to return before the surgery was over.

Grabbing a cab outside the hospital, she used the time on the way to apartment to call Les. He would have to juggle appointments until she got back to the office. Then she called Sam. He was still at the park, and thought he would be there most of the day.

Maggie was waiting in the hallway instead of sitting in

the waiting room, when Janet returned. "She's in recovery. Dr. Jordan said it went well. Let's go get a cup of coffee."

Strong and not too flavorful, they both sipped the vending machine coffee out of habit. "What do you know about Jenna?" Maggie asked.

"Not much. From the two conversations we had, I learned that she had a disagreement with her father when she was 17. After staying with friends and relatives for intervals, she decided to head to the city. She didn't realize how expensive it was to live here, and ran out of funds fast. I think she had some bad experiences since she arrived in the city. That's why she is such a loner. Staying away from all the drugs and prostitution is one of her biggest concerns. She's had a few jobs, but quit when people became overly friendly. That's a problem when you are young, pretty, and all alone."

Maggie listened while she sipped her coffee, not saying much.

A nurse came to get them. Jenna was groggy, but breathing much better. Concerned because Jenna refused to take any pain medication, the nurse hoped Janet would help.

Warily, Jenna watched Maggie. Janet introduced them. "This is Maggie Henderson from the police department. She's here to make sure you are safe. Maybe she could ask you a couple of questions?"

Maggie could see that Jenna was not ready to talk,

especially to her. "Hi! Jenna. I'll be right outside if you need me. We'll talk later." She hoped Janet would get her to talk.

Watching Maggie leave, she told Jenna, "Maggie is a real nice lady. She won't hurt you."

Nodding her head, Jenna couldn't explain to Janet how many people frightened her. Her instinct was to shy away from most new people she met.

Before they could talk, Dr. Jordan came into check on his patient. "Hey, sunshine." She was breathing so well that they only had a tube in her nose. Sal checked it. "Are you having any difficulty breathing?"

"No, my lungs feel heavy, but I don't feel breathless like I did." She said quietly.

"You are one lucky lady. From what I hear the Doc saved your life. If they had found you much later, I wouldn't have had a chance to get to know you better."

Jenna looked at Janet, then back at Sal. "Thank you both. I know you gave me a second chance to do something with my life. I won't let you down."

Janet watched as he examined her. Jenna responded to him like she had known him her whole life. Knowing how hard it was for Jenna to trust people, Janet was worried that Jenna would read more into her new relationship with Sal than what he really meant.

"It won't hurt you to take something for the pain. You don't have to be a hero." He admonished her gently as he looked at her chart.

"I don't take drugs." She looked at him stubbornly.

Realizing how difficult it might be living on the streets to avoid the drug scene, he understood her fear. "I promise to give you only enough to take the edge off the pain so you can sleep. I won't give you anything addictive." He could see her stubborn look had not changed. "Do you trust me?"

Sighing in frustration, she nodded. "Yes."

"Good." Sal Jordan took the medicine the nurse brought in and made sure Jenna took it. He touched her hand, and then gave it a squeeze.

Janet stood by watching them in amazement.

"Doc, don't stay long. She needs to sleep." He smiled at Janet. "You can come back later, if you like."

"Thank you." Janet followed him to the door and whispered. "If you are serious about Jenna, go slow. If you are just flirting, back off. She is very vulnerable and takes everything you say seriously. She already thinks she's in love with you."

Sal Jordan looked at her guiltily. "You are much more than a psychiatrist, aren't you?"

"I just see things that others don't."

"You are a good friend. I like her a lot, but I promise that I will give it a lot of thought before saying or doing anything. Jenna is too special." He smiled at Janet before closing the door.

As Janet came back towards Jenna's bed, Jenna yawned and tried to get more comfortable. "Dr. Janet, am I pretty?"

Smiling, Janet had to suppress a laugh. "Sure you are. Would you like to look in a mirror?"

Jenna made a face at her. "You are just being nice."

"We're friends, right? I only tell my friends the truth.

You are very attractive. But, we could fix you up a bit, add some makeup, and fix your hair." Janet thought this would be fun.

"Will you help me?"

"Sure. Do you remember me telling you about my friend, Les, who is in the theatre?"

Jenna nodded.

"When you wake up, you have the nurse call my office. We'll bring you a nice nightgown and do a complete make over. Les will show you how to do your make up and hair. He's much better at it than I am, and you'll love him."

"Is he your boyfriend?"

Janet laughed. "No, he's my best friend, more like a girlfriend."

Jenna laughed at that.

"Let's talk about what happened for a few minutes and then I'll clear out so you can sleep."

"I got up to go to the bathroom and had to walk a ways to find one that was unlocked. They lock most of them up at night. I was crawling back into my bed when he grabbed me. I fought with him until he stabbed me. It was so dark there under the trees. He had on a down jacket, and I think I knocked off his glasses."

"You sure it was a man?"

She nodded. "He pressed up against me when we were fighting." Jenna blushed a pretty pink.

"Anything else you remember?"

"Yes, he was breathing hard, sort of raspy. It sounded like Rhoda, a girl who worked at the deli. She had asthma attacks every once in a while."

"Good. Let me know if you think of anything else." Janet covered Jenna up better. "Get some sleep. I'll see you later."

Jenna fell asleep quickly. Janet left her business card by the phone. Maggie was waiting for her in the hall. Janet called Sam while Maggie listened so she wouldn't have to relay the information twice. She let Maggie talk to him then.

Curious, Maggie handed back the phone. "You two are serious?"

Janet nodded sensing that Maggie had been interested in Sam.

"Don't worry. We only went out once. I'm happy for you."

Janet could see that she was sincere. "Thank you! I have to get to work. I'll be back later. Call me if you need me."

Les had rearranged some of her appointments hoping she would be back by 10:00 and she got there at 10:15. Les brought in coffee. "O.K. Give me the condensed version."

Janet smiled and sipped the coffee gratefully. Les made good coffee. "I woke up with a start in the middle of the night." She told him every detail as quickly as possible.

Vicki Long

"Wow! You have been busy. I'll run out at lunch and pick up a few things including your lunch. I rescheduled one appointment at lunch; I hope you don't mind?"

"No, that's fine."

Les went to send in the first patient. Janet's day seemed to fly by. It was after 4:00 when Jenna's nurse called. Les promised they would be there by 6:00.

Janet went into the room first since Jenna hadn't met Les. "You look much better than you did this morning. You aren't so pale. Is it O.K. if I bring Les in?"

Jenna smiled and nodded. After she was introduced to Les, she asked excitedly. "Are you going to make me beautiful?"

Les smiled at Janet, and then made a big thing over looking at Jenna's hair and face. "I see potential here. What are we going for? Do we want to show off your natural beauty or do we want to knock his socks off?"

"We want to knock his socks off." Janet replied for Jenna.

Jenna smiled. While she was waiting for them, the nurse had helped her clean up. Jenna was very particular about staying clean, not an easy task living on the streets.

Les got out a pair of scissors, and glanced worriedly at Janet when he saw fear on Jenna's face. "You have beautiful hair. I promise to only trim the split ends unless...you say it is O.K. to cut more. I won't do anything you don't want me

156

to do. I want to be your friend."

Embarrassed by her reaction, she smiled at him. "I don't know. We'll let Janet decide."

"Pressure, pressure. O.K. Les is right. How about we taper it a little in the front to accent your pretty face?"

"I guess we need to go all the way to knock his socks off." Jenna blushed when she realized what she said.

Les looked at her, and then at Janet. "She's a virgin. You are a rare one. How could you live on the streets and stay a virgin?"

"It wasn't easy."

Janet gave her a proud look, which made Jenna raise her chin instead of hiding behind her hands. "I admire you, that takes spunk."

"Thank you." Jenna accepted Janet's hug, holding onto her for a moment. It was nice having friends.

Les started cutting her hair, talking to her so she wouldn't get nervous. "So, what is this doctor like?"

"Dreamy. Dark hair, curly and a little long in the back, nice eyebrows, a little five-o-clock shadow, and a hint of dark curly hair peaking out of the top of his shirt."

"Wow! Does he have a brother?"

Both Jenna and Janet giggled.

"What? As if you didn't know." Les continued to work his magic on Jenna, nothing drastic, just enough to accent what was already there. About a half hour later he stood back and looked at her. "You look great!" Les praised his own handiwork.

Janet was surprised at how beautiful Jenna looked. She handed Jenna a mirror. "What do you think?"

When Les went to take the mirror back, she pulled him into her arms for a hug. "Thank you."

It was Les' turn to blush. "You're welcome." Packing up his things, Les turned to leave. "Got to go, ladies. I'll see you both tomorrow."

As he was leaving he caught a glimpse of Jenna's doctor coming down the hall, and couldn't wait to hear how their little plan worked.

Sal entered Jenna's room a few minutes later, and did a double take. "Jenna?"

"Hi! Sal." Jenna blushed and smiled.

Janet was pleased to see his reaction, and left the room without them even noticing.

"Did you do all of this for me?" He asked, not taking his eyes off of her.

"Yes." Jenna's heart was pounding. Never had she felt this way, her body tingling with excitement.

"I'm not supposed to become involved with my patients you know."

"Then, you'd better help me get better so I can get out of here."

"Where will you go?"

With a deep sigh, Jenna admitted. "I have no where to go."

"Will you let me help find you a place?"

"But, I don't have any money."

"I'd loan you the money." Before she could object, he continued. "Janet can help you find a job. You could take some classes."

He painted a rosy picture. "Would I live alone?"

"Do you want to live alone?"

"No."

He was trying to understand her fear. She had lived on the streets everyday, all alone. "We could find you a roommate."

Her eyes spoke volumes.

His heart was pounding as he took her hand. Looking deep in her eyes, he couldn't seem to break away. "Doctors make terrible roommates. Phone calls in the middle of the night. Long shifts away from home."

"Roommates are also good to come home to, instead of an empty apartment."

"I'm too old for you."

"I'm 22, and you aren't even 30 yet."

"We'll talk about that again some other day. I do own the building where I live and there is an empty apartment. You can stay there.

When they heard the door open, Sal put his hand on her

wrist like he had been taking her pulse. Winking at her he put his stethoscope in his ears and listened to her lungs. A smile came to his lips when they sounded clear. "Let's do some tests to make sure you are healing properly. I'll think you will be able to go home soon."

Jenna liked the idea of going to live in Sal's building. "Great!" The nurse left to order the tests, taking the chart with her.

Sal touched her cheek. "I'll stop back before I leave tonight."

"Sal." She stopped him. "I've never been with a man." After blurting that out, she watched for his reaction.

"Really? Wow!" He smiled, admiring her. "Well, I think we need time to get to know each other a lot better before we go down that road. When the time is right, you will know it."

Jenna could hardly keep her hands off of him now. It would be right with him. She didn't want to hide from the world anymore. Jenna was ready to start living.

The next day Les stopped to see her at lunchtime. Jenna was so excited to see him. He showed her how to put on makeup like he had done the day before. "So, I guess everything went well last night."

"Yes, thank you so much. At first I was afraid he was just being nice to me, but he really does like me."

Les was glad she wasn't disappointed.

"Would you do me a favor? Would you ask Dr. Janet if she knows anyone who is hiring? I need to get a job." Jenna pleaded with him.

"Just any job? What kind of job would you be interested in? What skills do you have?" Les wanted to help her.

Panic returned to Jenna's eyes. "I don't know. I'm good with numbers. In high school, I took business courses, but that was a few years ago."

"I have a friend that has a book store who needs some help. He's looking for an assistant that can wait on customers when the store is busy, put away new books, and help with the bookkeeping side of the business." Les was testing her.

Jenna swallowed her fears. "That would be great! Should I call him to set up an interview?"

"I'll talk to him when I see him tonight and see if he'll give you a chance to try out the job." Les smiled at her enthusiasm.

"Thank you so much. Please tell him that I want to take some classes, that I'm willing to study hard and learn whatever it takes for the job."

"I'll do that." Les assured her, kissing her cheek. "Got to go. Janet will stop by after work. I'll see you tomorrow."

She stopped him with her words spoken mostly to herself. "I've wasted so much time. Now I have a second chance to live."

"You should be proud of yourself. I know Janet and I are

proud of you."

She was embarrassed that he heard her, but grateful. "Really?"

"Really." With a wave, he was out the door.

Jenna asked the nurse for books or magazines to read. She didn't want to waste another moment. There was so much to learn, to catch up on.

It was almost 7:00 when Janet got to the hospital. The previous day had put her behind, and she had stayed late to catch up with all her appointments. Les had dropped back by the office with a shopping bag for Jenna. He was enthused about Jenna 'coming out' and didn't want her to wait for what he had in the bag.

Jenna was sitting propped up in bed. She must have been dozing. Her eyes sprang open when she heard the door. "Dr. Janet. It's good to see you." When she saw the bag her eyes lit up. "Please tell me you brought me something to read. All they seem to have around here is fashion magazines or books that are so old. I want to improve my mind, not become a fashion model."

Laughing with delight at the transformation, Janet handed her the bag. "I didn't look inside so we'll both be surprised. Sounds like you will soon be ready to leave this place. You sound positively bored."

"Wow! Les is so cool." Jenna found two books on top some clothes. She pulled out two nightgowns, one bright pink polka dots and the other deep blue with tiny flowers. Also in the bag was a bright multi-colored kimono-type robe. Les' taste was a bit wilder than hers, but she liked how unusual everything was.

"Les likes to shop at second hand shops for his costumes. I was amazed the first time he took me to one how many of the clothes are almost brand new. It's like they hung in someone's closet for years and then someone else came along and cleaned out the closet."

Jenna smiled. "I hope the nurse will let me change into one of these tomorrow." She picked up the books. "Elizabeth Barrett Browning and a book on Bookkeeping." Sticking out of the first book was a piece of stationary imprinted with the name and address of a rare bookstore. The note read as follows:

> *Jenna,*
> *Les is a good judge of character, so the job*
> *is yours to try when you feel up to it.*
>
> *Come see me when you are ready to go to*
> *work.*
>
> *Your new boss,*
> *Jeff Stewart*

"Dr. Janet! He did it. Les got me a job." Jenna was so

happy that tears came to her eyes.

"Hey! You didn't cry when some weirdo stabbed you, but now you cry." Janet touched her arm in support.

"It's just that I'm so happy. I have you and Les for friends, a boyfriend, and now a job." Jenna smiled up at Janet.

"A boyfriend. Do tell. Has he kissed you yet?"

"Just on the cheek, but he finds all kinds of excuses to come see me."

"So, have you given any thought to where you will live when you leave here? You could stay with me in the spare room until you find a place."

"Thanks for the offer, but I'm going to move into Sal's building. There's an empty apartment. Today he brought me another doctor, a friend of his. He said he was too involved with me to be my doctor anymore."

Janet raised her eyebrows. "Sounds serious."

"You think so? I think I love him. It's all so scary and exciting at the same time. It's not what you think. He's not some guy that just wants to sleep with me. Sal said we had to get to know each other better before we move to that step in our relationship."

"I hope you are right. You need to take it slow. If you rush into all of this I'm just afraid that you may get hurt. You have my card. Promise to call me?" Jenna nodded and returned Janet's hug. "I've got to go. Sam is meeting me at our favorite restaurant for a late supper."

"The handsome detective?"

"Yes, the very busy, handsome detective. I've barely heard from him since we found you that night. You were the first victim to be found alive so you are the first one to give us clues about the identity of this murderer."

"He was here yesterday, and again today with Maggie. I wasn't much help. I couldn't remember much more than I told you. It was just too dark and it happened too fast."

"Well you have probably seen him more that I have. Bye dear." Janet kissed Jenna on the cheek and gave her a hug. After a quick wave she left.

Chris was actually the one who called her to tell her that Sam would be late and to meet him at the restaurant. When he arrived, Sam found Janet in the kitchen with George and his crew. She was decorating the top of a cheesecake with a jelly mixture in a pastry bag.

George greeted him first. "Sam, this lady is amazing. She just walks into my kitchen elbows one of us out of the way and does our job. What's so maddening is that she is good at it."

"It is so relaxing here. As soon as I get here, I feel like I'm at my Aunt Edna's house. She's been gone for 20 years, but I still remember how it felt to sit in her kitchen and help cook." After one final flourish, she put aside the jelly bag and went to kiss Sam.

George smiled. "That is the best compliment I've ever

received."

Sam could sense that she was a little angry with him. Tony took them to their favorite table, but she didn't say a word to him. When they were alone, she held out her hand. "Let me see your phone."

Janet punched in her cell phone number and let it ring several times without taking the phone out of her purse. Handing it back to him, she gave him a look that spoke volumes. "Pretty simple how that works, isn't it?"

"It was late when I got to the office last night. When I looked at the clock and saw how late it was, I didn't want to wake you. I actually fell asleep on a stack of files at my desk."

"Next time, call me. It doesn't matter how late it is. Hearing from you everyday really makes a difference. It's important to me." He looked worried. They never fought; after she made her point she felt better. She really missed him. Moving closer, she gave him a kiss that showed him just how much she had missed him.

Sam immediately saw the error of his ways. His body instantly responded to her kiss. When the waiter came, his face turned pink in embarrassment even if the waiter had no idea why.

He leaned over and kissed her again. "I haven't spent much time with you the last few days. You have every right to be mad at me. That was one of the reasons I wanted you to meet me here."

"I probably won't be much fun, I'm so tired." Sam warned her.

"You will be after you get some sleep." She smiled. "Just don't forget to call. I talked to Chris more this week than I talked to you."

"I promise." He looked deep in her eyes and then kissed her.

Janet smiled and hugged him close.

She asked him about the case. "Did you find any evidence at the scene?"

Sam smiled. "We found the knife, a common kitchen knife similar to the others. There were a lot of boot prints, but with so many people out there in the dark we think they belong to one of us. We did get one good fingerprint off the knife this time. There were two types of blood on the knife, Jenna's and the killer's. My guess is that he cut himself, slicing through the gloves he was wearing. It might have happened when Jenna was struggling to get away. The killer has been really careful up to now. This was a good break for us."

Sam was exhausted so Janet insisted that she take a cab home after they left the restaurant. He promised to meet her there again on Saturday. To make up for his lack of communication that week, he called her when he got in bed just to wish her 'good night'.

Chapter Twenty

For the next few weeks all was quiet again. Jenna was recovering quickly. She went home with Sal and moved into the apartment two floors below his. He had a loft on the top floor. Sal refused to do more than kiss her on the cheek until she was completely recovered.

As they got to know each other better, their feelings for each other did not change other than getting stronger. Sal had thought a lot about what Janet told him and decided he wanted to keep their relationship platonic until they were ready for marriage.

Jenna took the opportunity to start over and her independence very seriously. She began working in the bookstore, and went to the university to find out more about the classes that were available. Because of her financial situation, it would be several months before she could think about enrolling in any classes, but it was fun to plan for the future.

Wanting to give back to the community, she offered to help with Janet's shelter project. Since Sal was gone a lot, she had time to help.

Everything was set for the new homeless shelter to open. A retired teacher/missionary took over the management of the shelter. Janet retained the financial responsibilities.

Sam had one of his men continue to pose as a homeless person and befriend some of the others so he could find out where they went and where they hung out each day. After all the publicity, they had plenty of volunteers to work at the shelter including wives of local business moguls who considered the shelter the latest cause to make them look good with their socialite friends. There were a few misguided souls who were there to do community service. And then there were the real volunteers like Elizabeth, Sadie, and Jenna. They could empathize with the clients.

Jenna divided her time between the bookstore and the shelter. She was still a little shy around new people, but she worked tirelessly. On several occasions Sal came looking for her only to be put to work. Encouraged by Jenna, he set up a clinic in one of the rooms in the shelter for several hours two days a week.

Word spread fast among the homeless and the shelter was usually full. Counselors were urged to find other places for them to go instead of turning them away. Church basements and school gymnasiums were put to use if volunteer workers could be found to stay all night. Sam talked to some of the retired police officers, and helped her find new volunteers for these substitute shelters.

Not long after the shelter opened, Jenna started having problems. One particular volunteer, Andy Brinkman, came three times a week to work off his community service hours. He made a point of being there when Jenna was there. At first she thought he was just a coincidence, but when she changed her schedule, he changed his.

Of medium height and very thin, he had a very nerd-like appearance with his heavy-framed glasses. He didn't even say anything to her for several weeks, but after she worked in the kitchen with him a few times, he never seemed to shut up. He was always trying to impress her.

From the first day she met Andy, she felt very nervous around him. Because she was so shy, this was not so unusual, but in this case it felt different. It was like she had met him before, but she dismissed the whole matter as a figment of her imagination.

Only the problem continued to get worse. Andy started stopping by the bookstore. If she were in the office working, Jeff would tell Andy she was too busy to talk. But, if she was waiting on customers, she could not get him to leave. On several occasions he was rude to the customers she was waiting on. Jeff had told him to leave and he became very abusive.

Worried about her safety, Jeff told Sal about the problem. Jenna refused to quit going to the shelter so he went to talk to Janet. They changed her duties at the shelter several times and quit posting her schedule with the others. For several days she managed to avoid him. He started waiting outside after his shift was over and eventually caught up with her again. Fortunately, Les had stopped by to pick her up so they could go shopping.

Les flagged down a cab and was ushering Jenna inside. Andy pushed Les away and grabbed Jenna's arm to keep her from getting in the cab. Very athletic in build, Les was not the pushover people thought he was. With a good elbow shot to Andy's stomach, he extracted Jenna's arm from Andy's grip and pushed her quickly into the cab. Getting in beside her, he immediately called Sam on his cell phone.

A police car was sent to pick up Andy. They couldn't find him anywhere. Worried for her safety and on the chance that Andy was connected to the homeless murders, Maggie was assigned to stay with Jenna. Other officers were assigned to patrol the areas around her house, the bookstore, and the shelter, hoping to spot Andy. They staked out his workplace, his house, and a local bar where they were told he hung out. Background checks showed he had been in trouble several times. His current community service was for pushing a homeless person's shopping cart across a busy street, causing multiple fender benders, and a near miss when the poor man ran out into traffic after his cart. Andy became the first possible suspect since the murders began.

Stubbornly insisting that fear would not rule her life now when she had just started feeling good about her life, Jenna kept working both places. She did agree to change her schedule every week.

At least having Maggie go with her everywhere was better than having a uniformed policeman tailing her. They became good friends. Maggie had to check in several times a day so the police department would know where they were at all times. Jenna pretended not to notice.

Maggie liked books and enjoyed going to the bookstore with Jenna. As she learned the layout of Jeff's store, she started offering to help customers. Jeff offered to pay her for her time, but she could not accept anything in compensation. She was already being paid for staying with Jenna.

At closing time one evening while Maggie was in the restroom, Jenna asked Jeff the question that she had wanted to ask for quite a while. "So, you aren't like Les, are you?" How do you ask someone if they are gay without insulting him?

Jeff smiled and laughed. "No, Les and my brother have been long time friends."

"And, you like Maggie, right?" She would have been blind not to notice.

A redhead, Jeff blushed a bright red. "You think she knows?"

"I think you should tell her. Why don't you drive us

home? I'll fix dinner for all four of us?" Jenna felt like she owed both Jeff and Maggie so much. This was a way to pay them back.

"O.K." Jeff gave Jenna a hug.

That was the same day that Sam found out that Chris was dating Frannie. Janet was happy for them when she heard and invited them both to dinner that night. They had just started dessert when they got the phone call.

Jeff was leaving Jenna's apartment building, when he found a woman's body on the front steps of the building. Hitting the buzzer, he called and asked for Sal to come downstairs. She was barely alive. Jeff called the ambulance on his cell phone while Sal tried to help her. Maggie called Sam.

Janet insisted on going with Sam and Chris. Frannie said she would clean up and then take a cab home.

When they arrived Sam saw Sal cover the body with a blanket. He shook his head. "She had lost too much blood by the time we found her here. This one did not go to the shelters. She was so thin. Her body didn't have the strength to fight for life."

Janet stood back and closed her eyes. "I don't know this lady. She must not go to the park either. Turning around slowly, she stopped to look across the street. "I can feel him watching us. He's found a place to hide where he can watch us. I think he is on the rooftop across the street.

Sam and Chris went in Sal's building and out a back door to circle around before crossing the street. Chris called for backup units to quietly move in from the rear and check the surrounding buildings. By the time they made it to the rooftop, the killer was gone. They did find the blood-covered knife, confirming that Janet had been right.

After the ambulance left, they all went back to Sal's apartment. Maggie had kept Jenna in the apartment away from the windows. She had been worried, so she was grateful to see everyone safe. Sal gave Jenna a hug for reassurance while Sam and Chris filled in the rest of the details. Jeff had pulled Maggie into his arms for a hug, which caused Chris and Sam to exchange a smile.

Sal brought them back to the case at hand, because of his concern for Jenna. "Why do you think the killer would dump the body on our doorstep?"

Janet had been wondering about the same thing. "Do you think Andy is trying to tell us he is 'Homeless Harry'? Was this a copycat murder done by Andy to scare Jenna? Or, is the real 'Homeless Harry' trying to tell us he is still out there chasing down the homeless and killing them?"

"Whether the killer is Andy or someone else, he seems to be daring us to capture him." After looking at the others he asked. "Do you think we should tell everyone that Homeless Harry is Andy? We could put his picture in the newspaper. If Andy is not serial killer, he will either contact one of us or he will panic and run. That might solve Jenna's problem. If he is the killer, he will just continue on with his cause until he is caught."

"If Andy is not the real 'Homeless Harry', Harry may get even more upset because he doesn't want to share the credit for the murders. In that case, we would be daring him to commit another murder or to get Andy himself."

Chris jumped on that theory. "Why don't we run with it, publishing Andy's picture may smoke Andy out? All we have to say is that Andy is wanted for questioning in connection with the homeless murders. The press will take liberties and do the rest. Worst case the real killer could get so angry that he will start making more mistakes. Either way he isn't done murdering the homeless. I think we have nothing to lose."

After more discussion, everyone agreed with the plan. Sam would run their plan by the Chief before going to the newspapers. He wanted to do it right away as timing could make a difference. Even though it was late, he called their boss at home. The chief agreed with them that they really didn't have much to lose. Sam called some of his friends in the media. Chris volunteered to email a photo to the newspapers so they could make the morning edition.

Over breakfast the next morning, Janet read the newspaper and flipped through the TV channels to see how many networks had picked up the story. Sam called her. "The police stations are already getting phone calls. Most of the calls will turn out to be dead ends."

Janet was still hopeful. "I don't think we will have to wait very long. If the killer is going to react to the publicity, it will happen soon."

Chapter Twenty-one

For several days after that the same image, a symbol, kept popping up as Janet made her notes on her patients. Flipping back a few pages in her drawing pad, she slowly brought the image to life on paper. She hadn't seen it before, but knew it was important. After several days of doodling the same symbol across that page, she gave it to Les and asked him to try to figure it out. He liked doing the extra and the unusual projects that came up every once in a while.

He did not disappoint her. By the end of the day he brought her a story about the symbol, an Irish Claddagh. The story was of a man from the Village of Claddagh who was about to be married, but was captured by pirates and sold to a Moorish goldsmith. Once he was trained in the craft, he fashioned a ring with two hands holding a heart and crown. When he was released, he returned to his village and gave the ring to his beloved who had remained faithful and was still waiting for him. The Claddagh became the symbol for friendship, loyalty, and love.

Janet tried to remember what might have happened

just before the time the first image started pestering her subconscious. After all of her patients had left for the day, she sat back in her chair and closed her eyes. Mentally she reviewed the events over the last few days.

Suddenly, she sat up and knew why the symbol was important. Two days before, she had gone with Sam to the coffee shop where many of the police and detectives hang out. Sam had introduced her to an old friend, his father's old partner. What was his name? Shaunessy, but they called him Red. He wore an unusual ring. Over lunch they were talking about Red and Bill, Sam's dad, being partners and how they were together the night Sam's dad was killed. Janet stared sadly into space knowing Sam would not like her for what she now knew.

Being absorbed in her thoughts, she did not hear the front door open and close. She was surprised to see Sam come into her office. Les had left long ago, so she could only assume Sam now had a key to her office. Still stuck on the bad image, she did not jump up and greet him as usual.

"Something is wrong. What is it?" He walked around her desk and kissed her lightly. When she did not immediately speak, he sat in one of the chairs on the other side of her desk.

"I'm sorry." Janet got up and sat on his lap sideways to lean her head on his shoulder for a few moments. She drew comfort from his warm hands that held her. "Sometimes this gift of mine can be a curse. How was your father killed?" When he seemed reluctant to talk about it, she insisted. "It's important."

Sam sighed. "He was running down a dark alley after some punk kid and was stabbed." This was not something he liked to talk about.

"Did anyone ever find out who did it?"

"No, Red found Dad already down and there was no one in sight. They thought maybe the kid could have done it, but they never found him."

"Did you find the murder weapon?"

"No."

"What kind of weapon was it that killed him?"

"A switch blade, at least they think that was the weapon." Sam hoped she would get to the point soon.

"I believe that Red was the one who stabbed your dad."

Sam got up so fast that she fell to the floor before she could get her balance. "No way!"

Janet did not argue. She just got up and went back to her chair to sit. He did not look like he wanted her near him.

Standing at the window looking out for a long time, he finally said. "Show me." He went to her desk and picked up the drawings and notes that were spread across its surface. Each drawing was dated so he could see that she had worked this out over several days time. "Damn. How would I prove it?"

"Do you have a way to pull up a list of all the stabbings from say a year before your dad was stabbed until this year? We could say it's about the current case, if you don't want to tell anyone my theory." She offered.

"You think he's connected with the homeless murders?"

"No, not really based upon Jenna's description, but maybe he stabbed someone else. My instincts tell me that the homeless murders date back further than we think so we have two reasons for doing the research. If you can connect him to some other murder, you can confront him about your dad."

"Let's go!" Sam grabbed her jacket from the closet, and handed it to her as they walked out the door. He locked the office for her.

Once he was at his desk, Sam immediately pulled up the database and started a search. Janet pulled up a chair to sit where she could watch the screen. A curious clerk, Sue, came to see what they were working on and was immediately sent to start pulling the files as Sam's search brought in more results. They took the first 15 files including the one on his dad's murder into a briefing room to work.

When Sue brought more files, he asked her to order pizza and get some soft drinks for the three of them, handing her some cash. She came back with Chris and Maggie who had been looking for Sam. Without looking up, he told them what they were doing. "Janet believes that Red stabbed my dad. She also believes that it was not the only murder he committed. We are looking for any connection to that murder or the current ones. You two don't have to stay."

Sue was standing in the doorway with her hand out to Chris. "Do you guys want pizza? How many should I order? Two or Three?"

Chris gave Sue some money, looking at Maggie. She nodded. "Three."

Sue smiled and left to place their order. She liked helping with research, and often stayed late if there was something interesting going on.

They worked all night. Janet had her shoes off and both men had taken off their ties and rolled up their sleeves. She was the first one to speak in over an hour. "I keep coming back to this same file. A bookie was murdered. He often took bets from police officers. At the time of his murder, his associates believed he was killed by one of the police officers, but the man had so many other clients that could have been responsible for his death that no one ever investigated the possibility.

Chris had an idea. "Jim Jessup has been on the force all these years. I'm going to find him to see what he remembers." Grabbing his jacket and tie, he ran out. Maggie went to check the computer for gambling related deaths from that time period.

Sam started sorting the files by the date of murder to see

if any others were near that date. "Vaguely, I remember Red mentioning he liked to bet on football games. Dad wasn't big on gambling, but they often bet on who would buy donuts the next day. He was usually at our house to watch TV on Sunday afternoons. It seemed harmless fun at the time."

What happened next startled both of them. They were working quietly, looking through files when Red walked into the room. "Hey, Doc. I didn't know you were on the payroll?" It was not a pleasant greeting. "I knew you would be trouble."

Sam didn't like his tone. "What do you want? We're busy."

"All I wanted to do was retire and move into that small cabin on the lake that I bought a few years ago." He glared at Janet, but softened when he looked at Sam. "You can quit looking. It's true. Your dad found out that I was taking protection money to pay my gambling debts. Your dad found out about the bookie. I really didn't mean to kill that guy. We were arguing over some money I owed him, and he pulled a knife."

Red walked to the side of the table closer to Janet. Sam warned him to stop, his gun already pulled, but out of sight below the table.

"Your dad was trying to warn me that Internal Affairs was asking a lot of questions. He said that Internal Affairs had asked to talk to him in the morning. I panicked. My gambling debts were piling up and I didn't want to lose my job."

"You were his best friend. I'm sure he was only trying to help you." Sam challenged him, the grief as strong as it was the day his dad died.

"I know that now. Nothing was the same after that. I quit gambling, quit drinking, and straightened up."

"That won't bring him back." Sam wanted to pull his gun on Red, but had to think of Janet's safety first. When Red reached inside his coat, Sam's raised his gun quickly before he could draw his. Red held the gun loosely and laid it on the table. He slid it towards Sam. Next, he took out his badge, looked at it sadly, and then put it on the table.

From an inside pocket he pulled out a switchblade, flipped it open once quickly, closed it, before sliding it across the table to lie beside his gun. Finally, he took out his handcuffs. "We don't need these do we?"

"You bet we do." Sam motioned to Chris who stood in the doorway with Maggie with their guns drawn. Chris moved forward to put the handcuffs on Red. Maggie moved between Red and Janet, keeping her gun on him. Sue and many other officers stood in the hallway. Most had heard at least part of the Red's story and had their weapons drawn and ready.

After they took Red away, Janet dropped into the nearest chair. She hadn't moved since Red came into the room, thinking it was safer to let him forget she was there. Taking a big breath, she sighed in relief and looked at Sam to see how he was doing. Putting his gun away, he came around the table and sat heavily in the chair next to hers. "Are you O.K.?"

"Yes, how about you?" She leaned towards him and kissed him lightly.

Sam glanced across the table at the switchblade, and then lowered his face into his hands. As he started sobbing, she put her arm across his back and stroked it. Finally, he sighed and taking out his handkerchief dried his eyes. "Sorry."

"What for? You needed to grieve, nothing wrong with that. I would have been more worried if you hadn't cried." Getting up, she found her shoes and put them on. "Let's go. You need to get some sleep."

"No, I need to take care of a few things." He objected.

Maggie came back in the room. "No, you don't. We'll take care of it."

"Don't you need to get back to Jenna?" He was feeling mean.

"Sal is off all week." She met his angry stare defiantly.

Janet squeezed his arm. Looking quickly at her with the same anger, he slowly softened.

Putting his arm across Maggie's shoulders, he forced a smile. "Call me later with an update, O.K.?"

"You bet." Maggie admired Sam, and had asked to be

transferred to his department permanently.

They went to her apartment. With their clothes still on, they lay on the bed together. Sam held onto Janet tightly, gathering strength from her.

Sam sighed. "Dad would have loved you." Cuddling against her, Sam finally slept.

Janet slipped out of bed to go to the bathroom, and heard her cell phone ring. Grabbing it quickly, she took it into the living room.

Chris called her to check on Sam. "He's finally sleeping."

"I'm sorry. I probably woke you."

"No, I couldn't sleep."

"Red shot himself about a half an hour ago."

"What?"

"No one frisked him. He had another gun. We were getting ready to take him to be arraigned when we heard the shot."

"Wow!" That was all she could think to say.

"Don't wake him." Chris replied.

"O.K." Janet replied before Chris hung up.

"Call me if you need anything."

"O.K."

Janet stood at the window for a long time with the phone still in her hand. He found her there an hour later. Walking up behind her, he pulled her against him and wrapped his arms around her. Noticing the phone in her hand, he felt the tension in her body.

"Red shot himself. He's dead."

Sam looked out the window over her shoulder. Pulling her tighter against him, he said nothing. It was all like a bad dream. Surprisingly he felt better, like he finally had closure. His father's death had bothered him for so long.

Looking at him apologetically, she pulled away. She tried to explain. "I need to take a walk in the park." Needing to get some fresh air, she also wanted to forget about Red.

She talked Sam into walking to the park from her building. Before they left he dug a sweater out of the truck of his car to wear under his jacket. The sky was a dark gray. They weren't surprised when a light snow began to fall.

It was over an hour before either of them spoke. Janet had her drawing pad under her arm and Sam's hand in the other. "I should have stopped to pick up some blankets at the office." She said as she passed a bench where a homeless man had newspapers covering his shoulders.

"How many do you give out in the winter?" He asked.

"I bought 50 to give out myself."

Sam wanted to help. "I'll put out a collection box at the station.

"That would be great.

"I'll challenge my fellow officers to match your 50, bet you I hope we can collect twice that amount." Wanting to lighten their mood, he nudged her shoulder.

Smiling at him, she nudged him back.

Sam laughed. Stopping her, he went back to the homeless person they had seen. Returning without his sweater, he handed her the newspaper, which had her picture on it. "You are their hero. He didn't want to trade me. I told him that you wanted a copy of it for your scrap book."

"You are going to freeze, it's getting colder."

"No, but I'm hungry. Let's go home and order pizza. Do you have the ingredients for a salad?"

"Pizza, again?" Janet thought they needed something home cooked for a change. "I'll cook. I'm sure I can throw something together."

Chapter Twenty-two

Later that night, Janet gasped and sat up in bed. Grabbing the phone, she called Sam at home. "He's in the fountain."

Sam grabbed the phone on the first ring as he always did, but sat there rubbing his eyes, trying to wake up. "Who's in the fountain?"

"Andy." She gave him the location.

"I'll pick you up in five minutes." Sam hung up without waiting for her answer. While getting dressed, he called Chris to tell him to meet them there. Janet had pulled on her clothes from the night before and was waiting in front of the building.

When they arrived, Sam checked out the fountain with his flashlight. Andy was dead. He looked back at Janet and shook his head. He asked an officer to get lights set up around the scene.

Starting at the fountain, Janet walked around the scene in a circle pattern, trying to pick up on something, anything that may help. Finally she decided to sit on one of the benches nearby, but away from the commotion. As she moved closer to the benches, she noticed someone lying on a bench. There was no way anyone could sleep through all of the excitement. Shining the flashlight on the form on the bench, she noticed that the man was wearing Sam's sweater.

Leaning forward she checked the man's neck for a pulse, but found none. "Sam! Sam!" He was too far away to hear her, but another officer came running. She pointed to the body. "Please get Sam." Under the bench was a puddle of blood.

As Sam and several officers ran towards her, she stepped back out of the way. Touching Sam's arm to stop him, she whispered, "He's wearing your sweater. The killer was watching us yesterday. That poor man."

Sam moved forward to get a better look at the body, and then moved back to where Janet stood. She was waiting for him to come back, and he wanted to hear what she had to say.

Janet tried to keep her voice down. "This means the killer has made a connection between you, me, and this case. He is definitely following the publicity on the homeless and the murders. He doesn't like my interference and he knows you are on the case. The killer wants us to know that this is personal."

Sam looked straight at her so she knew he heard, but the FBI arrived. The local police were pushed back, while the FBI surveyed the situation. Sam stood with Janet and waited, knowing Lt. Cummings would be over soon to ask questions.

Lt. Cummings was surprised to see Janet. "What are you doing here, Doc? I told you to stay out of this."

"I'm involved in solving this case whether either of us likes it or not." She replied evenly. He hadn't even listened to what she had to say last time she tried to talk to him. Whether he believed her or not, it was not a reason to be rude.

Sam defended her. "Janet is the reason we are here so soon. She woke up and knew that Andy was in the fountain. She called it in and here we are."

"How do we know she didn't put him there? For all we know she could be the killer." Lt. Cummings replied and immediately regretted baiting Sam.

Sam was angry, and would have said a lot more, but Janet put her hand on his arm to stop him.

Lt. Cummings admired Sam's control and quickly backed off. "What about this other guy?"

Janet stubbornly glared at Lt. Cummings. "I found him after we got here. It seemed odd that he hadn't moved with all the excitement."

The Lieutenant nodded and went back towards the bench for a closer look. Walking back to them slowly, he decided to believe in Janet. "So, did you pick up on anything since you arrived, anything on the killer?"

"No, that is why I was going to come over and sit on a bench. I was hoping to get away from everyone and concentrate."

"Probably too many people here now. Looks like a three ring circus." Lt. Cummings said as he walked towards the fountain taking Sam with him.

Janet stood still looking around her. As a breeze blew by, the short hairs on her neck bristled. Feeling like they were being watched, she walked a few paces in either direction to try to sense his location. Flipping back the cover of her drawing pad, she tried to sense the landmarks around them, hers and his, to pinpoint his location.

Chris saw her trying to draw in the dim light and turned his flashlight on her drawing pad. Moving behind her, he directed the light over her shoulder and watched her draw. He had to resist the urge to turn around as he saw what she was drawing.

Luckily his phone rang. Sam had seen him standing with her and was calling to ask him to stay with Janet. As quietly as possible he told him about the drawing. Keeping the line open, Sam told the Lieutenant. Local police and FBI that were outside of the park were directed to move in slowly to the location, but it was too late. They found the murder weapon where Janet had said he stood watching them.

Lt. Cummings took Sam's phone. "I need a description."

Chris gave Janet the phone. "I couldn't see the details of his face. I think he's wearing a hood. He's about the same height as you, but thinner, a lot thinner. He wears glasses like Jenna said. If she is right, he is asthmatic. His clothes were dark, blue or black so I couldn't see the details. He wears sneakers, the old kind like we wore when we were kids. His face is very pale, a sharp contrast to his dark clothing. That's it."

He quickly briefed his sergeants who relayed the information to the others out searching.

A homeless lady who was upset about the police searching every inch of the park sought Janet out. He watched from afar as she called the shelters to find room for the lady for the night. Walking her to the street, Janet hailed a cab and paid the driver to take her there to make sure she arrived safely.

Several hours later, they had found nothing. Janet and Sam left once the evidence from both crime scenes was collected and the bodies taken away. Sam dropped her off at the apartment on his way to the office.

A few weeks later, Lt. Joe Cummings called and asked if they would meet him for dinner. Explaining that he had a new girl friend, he said he wanted her to meet both Janet and Sam. He said that Michelle was a social worker.

That night at dinner, Michelle talked about 'Chas' as she had nicknamed him and avoided all questions about herself.

She told them that Joe was just too common for such an important man so she called him 'Chas' after his middle name of Charles.

Janet spent most of the evening trying to figure Michelle out. She wasn't the most attractive woman, but seemed nice enough. There was just something about her that bothered Janet. Michelle squinted a lot like she should be wearing glasses. She was tall and thin, but not shapely. The evening went well and they went their separate ways after dinner.

It was several hours later when Janet realized why Michelle seemed oddly matched with Lt. Cummings. Turning on the bedside lamp, she called Sam. "Sam. Michelle is really a Michael. She is really a he. Joe Cummings is dating Homeless Harry. I'm certain of it. Just think a minute. Getting close to all of us without us knowing who he is would be the ultimate coup. He had to have known that I would figure it out eventually. Do you think he wants to be caught? Or, is he just playing a game with us?"

Sam was quiet, trying to wake up and absorb the bazaar idea she just presented. This was a lot to think about in the wee hours of the morning. "You're sure about this?"

When she told him she was sure, he told her to get dressed and meet him in front of her building. While he got dressed, he tried to call the Lieutenant on his cell phone. When there was no answer, he called the office and found out he was staying in a hotel several blocks from the police station.

While driving to Janet's building, Sam called Chris and gave him the address. Chris called dispatch to roll out other units without sirens. They didn't want to announce themselves until they were sure of the situation.

Only one unit had arrived by the time Sam and Janet pulled up out front. The hotel manager was called out by the front desk clerk when the uniformed officers entered the lobby. Sam and the officers took the elevator first and asked Janet to follow in a few minutes with the manager.

Knocking on the room door, Sam said, "Room service." No sound came from the room. After a few minutes, he tried again. "Police. Open the door." When there was still no response, the manager unlocked the door for them. With guns drawn, they moved slowly into the room.

Lt. Cummings was naked on the bed, lying on his back, one hand cuffed to the bed. He had been stabbed and the knife was still in his chest. Sam reached over to check for a pulse, but found none.

Sam was still having a problem believing that the killer would fool the Lieutenant so easily. Was Michelle really a Michael? If so, she or he sure fooled all of them, but Janet. Sam looked back at Janet. He had no reason to doubt her.

It was just such a crazy idea. She watched them as they gathered evidence. There wasn't much in the room, only his clothes and his toiletries in the bathroom. No glass or beverages or any sign that anyone else had been in the room. No one was able to find even a fingerprint.

Before they zipped the body bag, Janet called out to them. "Make sure you check for DNA."

All eyes were trained on her in confusion. Sam looked at her in disbelief. "You think that the killer gave him a blowjob?"

"No, I think that Michelle did before showing him she was really a Michael to add to his humiliation. Did you see all the bruising on the arm that was cuffed? He probably freaked out when he found out Michelle was Michael. I think he would have been shocked at such a challenge to his masculinity and tried to get loose. He would want to get as far away from Michael as possible, or want to violently attack him."

Sam nodded towards the coroner who covered that area of the body with plastic before zipping the bag. No one in the room spoke for a long time. None of them could conceive the scene she had painted for them, although they had no reason to doubt her.

Chris left to go find Lt. Cummings' car and to look through the office he was using at the station hoping to find a phone number, address, or other information. No briefcase or notes had been found in the room, and they knew he carried a big black briefcase.

Other officers made inquiries around the hotel to see if

anyone had seen Michelle/Michael leave the hotel. One desk clerk remembered them arriving together, but no one had seen him leave.

"The problem is that we do not have a picture to show anyone." Janet sat down in the lobby to work on a sketch of Michelle, hoping to create one of Michael afterwards. Her memory was pretty good on faces, and she drew a good likeness of Michelle. As she tried to draw Michael, she struggled for several minutes. At one point it suddenly got easier to draw him. Without looking she knew he sat directly behind her. Not wanting to miss this opportunity, she waited to speak until the drawing was done.

"Do you want to turn yourself in?" She asked quietly while her eyes searched the room for Sam or Chris.

He laughed, but was not amused. "No, actually I'd like to take you and Sam out of the picture. Then I can go back to living my life normally."

"You think normal is killing people. Why do you hate the homeless so much?"

He spoke freely to her. "My mom was a social worker. She would go out on the streets every evening and help the homeless. Kind of like what you do only it was her job. One of them slit her throat with a knife."

"Maybe it wasn't a homeless person? Maybe it was some gang member or druggie, or just someone like you?" She could see the hotel manager looking at her. She mouthed,

"Get Sam. Get help!" He seemed to understand as he picked up the phone and started punching in numbers.

"You think you are so smart and that you have all of the answers. Life is not that simple. Let's go for a walk. Just you and me."

He grabbed her arm to pull her from the chair, but she resisted hoping to get the manager's attention. "I'm not going anywhere with you." She raised her voice and fought to release the grip he had on her arm.

Sam and two other officers came running towards them.

Michael saw them, pushed her away and fled. A large group of businessmen were leaving so he moved with the crowd out the front door. Officers ran after him, but found only the businessmen getting into taxis and limousines. Searching the area, they didn't see him. None of the people out front even noticed him or where he had gone.

Janet was shaking, but kept her cool. "Here, you'll need copies to help with the search." Sam took the drawing. The hotel manager offered to make copies.

Alone for a few minutes, Sam pulled her into his arms. "Are you sure you are O.K.? Did he hurt you?"

"I'm fine. Go! Find him!" She was more concerned with catching Michael.

"You stay with the manager. I'll ask Maggie to come get you." Sam took the original drawing and some of the copies and left to distribute them. After taking Janet into his office, the manager, Glen Kirby, called his own security and had copies distributed throughout the hotel. Within a half hour every on duty FBI or NYPD officer had a copy of the drawing and a citywide search was underway.

Glen Kirby stayed with her in the office. He was concerned for her safety and worried because she was so pale. He had someone bring a tray into his office and offered Janet some orange juice, coffee, and danish. By the time Maggie arrived, Janet was restless, anxious to help with the search in some way. She thanked Glen for all his help and promised to keep him informed on their progress.

Maggie laughed once they were safely on their way. "I think Glen Kirby likes you."

"He's a nice man. I think he was just concerned for my safety. Without his watchful eye and quick thinking, I might not be here. I still don't know how Michael ever imagined that he could force me to go with him in such a public place."

"His mistake, he should know you're too smart to fall for such a dumb stunt."

Janet quickly changed her clothes for work. Maggie objected. "Can't you take one day off?"

"No, I need to keep busy. Les can help if there is any trouble. He prides himself on having a tight fit body." Maggie laughed, and Janet smiled.

She was running late and hadn't called Les. Knowing he

would be upset, she told Maggie she wanted to hurry.

"What happened? Is everyone alright?" He followed them into the office. Janet told him quickly what had happened with as much detail as she remembered. Some of the story Maggie hadn't heard before. Janet gave him a copy of the drawing in case Michael came to the office, which she didn't think would happen.

For a few minutes all he could say was "Wow." But his quick mind soon kicked in gear. "Wait! Describe the type of clothes she was wearing. Maybe I can find out where she/he got them."

Janet made a face in doubt.

"Well, it is worth a try. At least I'll be doing something to help."

Tearing the drawing of Michelle out, she handed it to him describing the colors and fabric of the clothing as best as she could remember. Les went back out front.

Maggie hadn't said much. "Are you sure you are O.K?"

The determined look on Janet's face showed her how futile it was to argue.

Janet opened the door to the storeroom off her office. "You can sit right inside this door. That way my patients can't see you, but you will be able to listen in case something happens." Janet found a chair for her and told her she could ask Les for coffee or soda if she wanted some. "I'm afraid that is the best I can do. My patients won't talk to me if they know someone else is listening."

Maggie approved. "It will work." Not sure what she would do with all her time, she asked Janet for a legal pad. "I like to write song lyrics."

Later Les ordered lunch for all three of them. They sat in Janet's office to eat.

Janet remembered what Michael had said about his mom and told them. Maggie remembered one of the case files she had looked at and called Sue. They put the phone on speaker once she found the file. "Catherine Wilson was a missionary and social worker who worked with the homeless. According to the file she went out at night into the dark places where these people live. She would preach to them and pass out food and blankets. The file shows she did have a son. Give me a few more minutes and I'll see what I can find on him."

Sue continued to read from the file. "It was believed at the time that she was attacked by some drug dealer, not a homeless person. The boy saw the whole thing. He hid in a box or a dumpster." She paused for a moment while all they heard was the click of her fingers on the keyboard.

Les pulled out the phone book. There were 30 people listed with Wilson for a last name.

"Are there any Ms, Michaels, or Mikes?" Janet asked.

"Two Ms, one Mike, and one Michael." Les told them. He heard his phone ring and went to answer it at his desk. He was back in only a few minutes. "My friend at a shop on 52nd

Street says a guy matching that description bought a dress like the one in your drawing a few days ago. Look, this M. Wilson is on 52nd Street. It can't be more than a few blocks away from the store."

Sue came back on the line. "You were right, his name was Michael. Les, what is the address you found? I'm going to call Sam and Chris while dispatch sends a couple cars to check it out. I'll call you back."

Police units rolled out immediately. Chris and Sam were the first to arrive since they were not far away. Chris found the building superintendent and had him follow them up the stairs. When no one answered their knock, they had the super unlock the door. No one was in the apartment. Sam and Chris decided to stay and wait for a search warrant. Other officers were dispatched to patrol the neighborhood in cars and on foot to look for Michael Wilson.

They did not have to wait long for the search warrant. Making sure there were no marked patrol cars parked in front of the building, Sam and Chris went inside, closed the door and searched the apartment while they waited. If they got lucky, Michael would come home while they were there.

Sam searched the desk and found a scrapbook full of news clippings on all the murders and on the homeless. There were a lot on Janet, the homeless benefit, and the new shelter. Sam even found an article with his picture. At the very beginning of the book was a clipping about Catherine Wilson's murder.

Chris called to him from the bedroom. "Look what I found, a whole box of knives, no two are the same. Maybe he works at a restaurant supply company?

Sam went back to the desk and started looking for pay stubs. In one drawer he found five years worth of pay stubs from at least 20 different restaurants. Going through them as quickly as possible to find the most recent. "Chris, he was working at the Hilton at the time of the benefit. I bet he loved it when Frannie turned the kitchen inside out to feed all the homeless."

Chris came into the room looking worried. He called Fannie just to make sure she was all right. Surprised to hear from him during the day, she asked him if he was O.K. "We think the guy we are chasing worked at your hotel for a while, Michael Wilson. I just had to hear your voice."

Frannie was touched. "I'll ask around for information. Maybe I can get to his personnel records."

"Thanks. I'll see you later." He looked at Sam and shrugged. "Frannie is going to check with personnel.

"Well, the two latest pay stubs are from a diner called "Slam Dunk". Sam called two other plain clothes Detectives, and asked them to check out the diner while they continued to search the apartment.

Janet was the first to hear about Michael. The manager of her shelter, Sally Stemson, called her. "There's this guy holding everyone hostage. He's blocked the doors. Anytime now he is going to look in the office. Please call for help."

"What does he look like? Tall and very thin with heavy rimmed glasses?"

"Yes, how…?" Sally stopped suddenly.

Janet heard Michael yelling and the phone dropped

on the desk. He came back and dropped the phone on its cradle.

Immediately she dialed Sam's cell number. Maggie came running. "Sam, Michael is at the shelter. He's holding everyone there as hostage."

Sam and Chris went running to the car. Chris called into dispatch while Sam continued to talk to Janet. "Do you know how many people are in there?"

"No, but it's almost lunchtime. There could be as many as thirty - fifty people there. We'll meet you there." Maggie and Janet ran out, after telling Les where they were going.

Inside the shelter, Sam's undercover operative, Ed Capelli, was trying to make himself as inconspicuous as possible. He had a small microphone that they had given him. Until this point there had been no reason to use it. When everyone's attention was directed towards the gunman, he quickly turned it on and pinned in to his jacket. He hoped that they remembered he was in there.

Chris was still talking to the office when the car rolled to a stop outside the shelter. Looking over at Sam, he reported. "They believe that Ed is in the shelter. They are sending over a van with a receiver. If we are lucky, Ed will turn the microphone on."

While officers surrounded the building on all sides, Chris and Sam helped set up the van. Only minutes later they were listening to what was going on inside the building. Ed heard "we're receiving" through the earpiece he had slipped into his ear earlier.

Ed talked in a normal tone. "I'm hungry. I wonder if they are still going to feed us?"

"Heard you loud and clear." Chris responded.

While Ed and the others watched, one old man got up and walked quickly to the door. "I want to leave. I can't stay here." Going to the door, he began frantically moving the boxes Michael had stacked against the locked door. Without stopping him, Michael just watched the old man struggle with the boxes. When he had moved the last one, he looked at Michael and unlocked the door.

"Here let me help you with that." He offered, putting the gun in his pocket. Michael pulled the door open with one hand, and stabbed the old man with the other as he tried to run out the door. The man turned and stood still looking at Michael in disbelief for a moment before Michael pushed him out on the sidewalk and slammed the door. After locking the door, he rammed the knife into the nearest box. "That's what happens to anyone who gives me trouble."

Everyone was suddenly very quiet.

Outside the police tried to help the old man. First they carried him away from the building. One of the officers tried to staunch the flow of blood until the ambulance arrived. When they took him to the hospital he was in serious condition, but still alive.

Michael made another search of the kitchen and offices to make sure everyone was in the dining hall. Sally sat nervously on one end of the farthest table not far from her office. When Michael came out of her office again, he walked up to her. "What's upstairs?"

"The second floor is where we sleep, the volunteers and some of the clients. No one is supposed to be up there after 10:00 a.m. We clean early in the morning. No one is allowed upstairs until after 8:00 in the evening."

Michael nodded. He could see no reason to doubt her. After the incident with the old man he couldn't leave the dining hall to check it out himself. "When do you usually serve the noon meal?"

"From 11:30 until 1:30. That's why there are so many people here right now. Are you hungry?" Sally hoped that feeding everyone might prevent any more incidents like the one they had just witnessed.

Michael liked her, even if she was working with the homeless. She reminded him of his grandma. He nodded.

"Is it O.K. if we go ahead with our normal routine? It will calm everyone down."

"O.K." Michael watched her as she signaled to the two volunteers to come help her. He positioned himself on the dining hall side of the passageway between the kitchen and the dining hall where he could watch everyone.

When the food was all set in the steam tables, Sally

asked if he wanted to be served first. She filled a plate for him based upon his nodding or shaking his head at each entrée. He found a seat where he could watch the whole room and the door. Sally brought him a glass of milk and a cup of coffee. "Thank you."

"You're welcome." His positive response made her a little braver. "O.K., let's start a line, this table first."

As everyone filed through the line in an orderly manner and sat back down, the room became a little noisier. Sally was pleased to see that people were relaxing, even whispering amongst themselves. Filling her own plate she sat near Michael. This was a diplomatic gesture since he seemed to like her.

Ed decided to sit near two brutish looking men to enlist their aid. Neither of the men was open to conversation at first, even about the food. He tried a different tact. "What right does this guy have telling us what to do?"

"I've got a knife, too, but I don't go around slicing people." The dark haired burly looking one responded.

"Don't like knives. I was a black belt myself. Learned in the Navy." The blond guy who was built like a football player mumbled.

"I was in the green berets." Ed volunteered. "We need to find out how many others will help us get this guy. Can't let this guy go on stabbing people."

After a quiet conference, each of the men got up and

moved to a different table. Word spread quickly. Sally usually allowed people to go back for a second helping if there was anything left over. They were counting on this opportunity to make their move. Otherwise they would volunteer when Sally asked for help with the trays.

Sally finished her plate and got up to check how much food was left. Her two helpers came to help her. Walking back to Michael, she offered to get him a second helping, but he declined. Walking back to the steam table, she announced, "First come first served for seconds."

Only 13 men and 1 woman got up and moved towards the front of the dining hall to stand in line. As Ed moved toward the line, he said into his microphone, "We're going for it."

They were ready to move in as soon as they got the signal. Chris alerted the other police officers and they approached the building. Maggie and Janet stayed in the van to listen to Ed's transmission.

Inside the shelter, Michael had finished eating and brought his tray up to the steam table moving to the front of the line that was forming. This was the break Ed was hoping for. Moving quickly he brought his tray down on Michael's head yelling, "Go!"

Pulling his knife, Michael frantically stabbed at anything within reach. It took six of them to wrestle it away from him, a few receiving nasty cuts as payment. The woman that came forward with the men to get in line for seconds ran to help Sally unlock the door, and then rushed outside to freedom.

Sam, Chris and the other officers rushed in, and a cry of relief rang out through the room. Many ran for the door.

Michael was handcuffed and half-dragged to a patrol car. Three officers rode with him on the way to the police station to make sure he did not get away.

Medics ran into the shelter to take care of the few that were wounded. None of the injuries were very bad, but a few were taken to the hospital for stitches. Ed thanked every one of them personally. "I couldn't have done it without you. Let me know if I can ever return the favor."

Several people came up to Sally and thanked her for handling the situation so well. Two ladies came up just to give her a hug, which brought tears to her eyes. She went over to one of the tables and sat heavily in a chair. One of her helpers brought her a cup of coffee.

Before everyone could leave, Ed announced loudly that Sally deserved some time off and that he was going to do dishes. "Anyone want to help?"

To his surprise, they began to clap loudly in appreciation for Sally's handling the situation so well. Ed began rolling up his sleeves and gathering trays. Some left, but there were several who stayed to help.

Janet and Maggie watched Michael being taken away, and then went into the shelter. They found Sally sitting down watching her friends clean up the dining hall with tears streaming down her cheeks. Gathering the woman into her arms, she held her while Sally let loose pent up emotions. A teenage girl that knew Janet came up to them. "You should have seen her. She was amazing, so cool and calm. If I volunteer will you let me stay here?"

Sally dried her eyes and blinked at the girl for a moment. "Sure. Janet and I will help you." This was what it was all about. Suddenly feeling better, she got up and danced the girl in a circle. "Thank you for volunteering."

They watched the girl walk off smiling towards the kitchen.

"There is someone in the kitchen you have to meet. He's the hero in all this. Can I keep him?"

Sally led Janet towards the kitchen. Going straight to the sink, she tapped him on the shoulder. When he spun around she grabbed him and hugged him as hard as she could. Then she pulled the tall man down to her level so she could kiss him on the cheek. She thought she could see his cheeks grow pink, but it was hard to see through his disguise. "Take all that crap off and let us see the real you." She demanded.

Grinning at Sally, Ed took off his sunglasses and his stocking hat, which had long shaggy hair attached to it, showing everyone his baldhead.

"I just wanted to thank you. You saved our bacon today." Sally said.

"Just doing my job." Ed assured her.

Two fellow police officers who came into the kitchen to refill their coffee interrupted the conversation. "Hey Ed, when are you going to become a real cop again. First you camp out on the streets, and then you start doing dishes."

Sally gave them a stern motherly look. "Better than sitting around drinking coffee." Neither one said a word.

Ed leaned down and whispered. "They were just teasing."

Sally smiled and whispered back. "I know. I'm going to give them each a dish towel and put them to work." Speaking louder, she introduced Janet to Ed.

He shook her hand. "I admire your hard work for such a just cause. I didn't realize how bad it could be until I took this assignment."

"Thank you for helping us catch Michael. It was a very brave thing to do." Janet liked Ed, too.

"Don't give me all the credit. My friends here helped. I couldn't have done it without them." He pointed to the two men helping him. Ed had just been talking to his two new friends about moving in with him. "I don't want any special credit for this unless everyone involved gets the same recognition." He smiled at his friends before giving them each a back slapping hug.

Janet understood why Sally wanted to keep Ed around. "I agree. Does this mean that you might consider being a regular volunteer around here?" She asked hopefully.

"You just try to keep me away." He grinned at her before turning back to the dishes.

Stitch, the young girl who wanted to stay with Sally, brought another woman over to them. She was about Janet's age with long tangled brown hair that framed a sad face. "This is my friend, Anne. We take care of each other. I've talked her into staying here with us."

Sally took Anne's hand and gave it a pat. "You are quite welcome."

Anne gave Sally a tentative smile before following Stitch back into the dining room.

Janet and Sally moved slowly in the same direction. "You know they can't stay here very long."

"Yes, but we'll take it one step at a time." Sally said optimistically.

Janet was relieved that Michael was in custody. It was ironic that the stunt he pulled that day actually helped get more homeless off the streets.

Sally insisted that she was fine when Janet tried to get her to take some time off, and that getting back to work was just what she needed. Sally was the one permanent resident at the shelter, having an apartment on the third floor. Being a missionary her whole life, she had always lived where she worked and really had nowhere else to go. Her husband had passed away many years ago and their only child had died shortly after birth. Between assignments she would stay with friends or a church would offer her a place to stay. All her possessions fit in her old station wagon, which was parked in the tiny garage at the back of the building.

"I'll be fine. It will be quiet tonight and I have Stitch and Anne to help me." She smiled as she watched her two new volunteers washing off the tables. "We've accomplished a lot today. I am truly thankful."

Janet chose not to argue. "Well, promise to call me if you need me for anything."

"Sure. Don't worry." Sally patted Janet on the hand that pressed hers, and then went back to work.

Maggie had been called away, so Janet took a cab home. She had called Les earlier to tell him what happened. He already cancelled her appointments for the rest of the day. Watching the rush hour traffic as it moved slowly, she decided to call Sam. "How is everything going?"

"Good. We put him into a private cell and he will be arraigned in the morning. Surprisingly, he hasn't said one word since we brought him here. A court appointed lawyer tried to talk to him, but he would not respond. I know he hears us."

"Do you think it's an act?"

"No. He's probably plotting some strategy to use what happened today against us in court. I'm going to try again this afternoon before I go home." Sam was guessing.

"Can he do that?" Janet hoped not.

"He may try anything since he is desperate, but he's guilty on so many counts that we should be able to put him away for the rest of his life." Sam hated to think what might happen if they had to release Michael.

"Well, I'm on my way home. Do you want to come over for dinner?"

"Sure, but it might not be until 7:00."

"No problem. See you then." Janet was anxious to see him.

Chapter Twenty-three

When Sam arrived he found Janet asleep on the sofa. Dinner was baking in the oven with the timer set. He sat next to her and watched her for a few minutes before kissing her.

"Wow, I fell asleep? I was just going to rest for a few minutes." Stretching, she pulled him back for another kiss.

He followed her into the kitchen and told her about Michael's interrogation. "He still wouldn't talk. His lawyer talked to him, and then I tried again." Loosening his tie, he pulled it off and hung it on a chair.

"Finally I slid a legal pad and a pen in front of him and told him I would go get him a cold soda while he wrote his confession. I told him it would be a long drawn out trial without his confession." I walked out and went for sodas. Before going back in I went into the observation room to take a look and saw him writing. His lawyer was watching him from there. Michael was already on the second page."

Grabbing another legal pad and pen I went back into the room. Michael paused to open the soda and take a drink, but then kept writing. He almost filled the legal pad with every murder he ever committed before putting the pen down. Chugging the rest of the soda, he went to the door to wait to be taken back to his cell. I asked if he had signed it, but he ignored me. The guard took him back to his cell. After making a copy for myself, I spent the next hour reading and making notes."

Chris and Maggie helped me compare the confession with the stack of cases that we had pulled as possible ones he committed. There were ten we didn't know about, three committed before we started our investigation, just like you suggested. We have a meeting with the District Attorney in the morning. Hopefully, we can get a court date soon."

Janet sat a platter of roast beef, vegetables and potatoes on the table and sat down across from him. Sam said grace, and they helped themselves from the platter sitting between them. It had been a long day and they both ate for a while in companionable silence.

Janet was thinking about the little boy, Michael, watching his mom being murdered. "Do you think he'll end up on death row or in some asylum?"

"A good lawyer might be able to get him put away some place for the criminally insane, but I think he will end up on death row. He hasn't shown any initiative towards fighting the charges against him so far." They talked about the case while they ate. Sam got called away again while they were clearing the table.

Janet's schedule became routine again, but Sam was so busy she rarely got to see him. Every case file and every piece of evidence was checked to make sure they were ready for court. Sam didn't want to risk anything going wrong.

Investigations were initiated on the other ten murders. One by one they found the bodies of the last seven, but the first three were now more than a year or two old. A lot can change in the city in that amount of time. He decided to ask Janet for help.

With Chris and Maggie plus two FBI agents, they went to an area at the far south of Riverside Park towards the ship docks. Michael had written in his confession that the body of a teenage girl was dumped in a cement culvert that looked almost like a grave vault without the lid. This was Michael's first victim. He wrote that he wanted to save her before she became a streetwalker or drug addict like many of the homeless teenagers. That was all they had to go on.

They searched the area one small section at a time visually. Janet would pause from time to time to close her eyes to try to absorb her surroundings mentally. In the 30's and windy, they had to keep moving to keep warm. After more than two hours, Maggie went to get them some coffee.

Returning, Maggie called out to Janet. She turned and saw something behind some bushes. This area was covered with fall leaves, but at the angle from where she was standing, she could see something sticking up. "Call Sam and Chris."

Maggie handed her the cup of coffee and did as she asked. Both ladies were kneeling down by the bush when the men found them. Janet moved out of the way when she heard them. Sam put on a pair of gloves and brushed the leaves away gently to reveal a red coat. Chris radioed the two FBI agents. Very carefully the team collected what evidence they could before moving the body.

"How did you find it?" Sam asked later.

"Maggie called out to me and I turned. Something caught my eye."

"Just luck, huh?" Her senses were so sharp that he found it hard to believe that it was only by chance she found the body.

"Yes, this time it was just plain old luck." They shared a smile.

Two days later the same team went out to look for the second victim's body. This one took some research. Michael had described the site as a large open grassy area surrounded by fir trees. There were three areas matching this description in the park, but they didn't have any luck finding even a trace. Chris had gone to the city planner's office and found out that there would have been another grassy area at the time of the murder; a large playground had been constructed there about six months earlier.

Maggie found it hard to believe that no one found the body during the construction. Sam could see her point, but Michael had mentioned the body was between two fir trees. When they arrived, they saw that there were ten tall trees thick with branches that grew all the way to the ground, providing lots of room to hide things underneath.

It was a slow, sticky and sometimes painful process to search the branches. Not sure what was important and what was not, they each put what they found in an evidence bag for examination later. Most of what they found was just litter. If nothing else they were helping to clean up the park.

Janet got up and brushed off her jeans. Something caught her mind's eye and she walked straight across the grassy area. This tree was much broader than the rest. Pulling apart several branches, she found the overhanging branches had formed a large natural shelter. It was almost high enough for her to stand upright in. Someone had threaded a tarp across a low branch to make a tent-like structure.

Stepping back and letting the branches fall, she was amazed at how invisible it all was from the outside. The others were watching her so she motioned them over to join her. With Sam pulling the branches apart on one side and Chris on the other, they all got a glimpse of what she had found.

Sam thought the best way to enter would be from the back. One of the FBI agents followed him and they crawled under the branches. While the others watched from the front, they pulled back the flaps of the tarp. Inside the opening was a body in a tattered flannel shirt and jeans. It looked like he had crawled back into the tent after he was stabbed. His body was laying in the opening with a dark trail running into the dirt outside. They took a lot of photos and looked for evidence. Hopefully, they would find something useful in the lab.

Through a search of missing person reports, they were able to identify the second victim. At the time of his death he had only been on the streets a short time. He had walked away from the Veteran's home where he was a patient. His family had made up posters to try to find him. A copy of the poster was on file, which made finding his family easier. Maggie contacted them.

The first victim was not as easy. The computer composite done by the morgue to help them with identification didn't match any missing person reports. No one wanted to believe that no one would be looking for such a young girl. To think that someone would not miss her was unfathomable.

Meanwhile, some unknown businessman who sympathized with Michael's grudge against the homeless hired him a lawyer, a hard-nosed lawyer who liked to work against the legal system. By convincing Michael that he too hated the homeless, he took on Michael's case.

For the first time since his capture Michael was talking,

but only to his lawyer, Jonah Craigmoor. Jonah arranged for Michael to see a Psychiatrist to prove he was insane, their only logical defense.

Sam's team and the FBI were working closely with the District Attorney to build a solid case against Michael. The D.A., Andrea Sole, also brought in a Psychiatrist to examine Michael. Jonah insisted that Michael had to talk to both Psychiatrists if he wanted to use the insanity defense.

Janet stayed out of the case unless they needed her help. With her practice, the shelter and her other projects she was very busy. Les heard that the office next door would soon be available. Janet negotiated for the space and got the contract.

Using a drawing that Janet did of the new office layout, Les met with several contractors to get estimates for remodeling. There was plenty of space for them to add one or two other doctors and space for a large room for group therapy.

Janet planned to take the small room closest to where her existing storage room was located and make it an extension of her own office. She planned on taking the wall out between and making the adjoining room into a file room. Using her drawings for patient notes made patient files often quite large so they needed a file storage room.

One remaining victim had yet to be found. Sam went back to Michael to ask for more details. A lot more sure of himself by this time with all the attention he had received from his lawyer, he just grinned at Sam.

"It's not for me. The family deserves to know what happened to the victim. They need closure." Sam pleaded.

"Your Dr. Janet passes by the body each time she goes to the park." That was all he would say. Sam had someone take him back to the cell.

Since it was cold, and often snowy Janet hadn't been spending as much time sitting in the park. Keeping moving to keep warm, she took a few blankets and some food with her each day and walked until she found the people who needed them. Sam told Janet he would bring a few blankets from the collection box at the station and walk with her at noon. He had asked Chris, Maggie, and the others to wait nearby. He wanted to talk to Janet alone. They would follow at a distance to help, if Janet led him to an area to be searched.

While they walked, he told her what Michael said. She tried to stick to her normal summer route. As they walked, they looked around.

"Who was the fourth victim?" She asked trying to get an idea of where to look.

"The fourth and fifth victims were found on park benches in the same section about a week apart." Sam showed her the area.

She had met many of her homeless friends in the same

area. "I walk by here almost every time I come to the park. Let's look around here."

Sam called Chris, Maggie and the other officers. Together they searched the area.

Maggie found a man's shoe laying under a tree, and the other one was found a distance away. "These could be from the body."

"Those shoes look way too new to be from a victim dead over a year now." Chris bantered back.

Janet smiled at Sam. Even though it was cold, she decided to sit on a bench for a few minutes to try to collect her thoughts. After asking if it was O.K., he sat next to her. "I wasn't sure if I would bother you."

Shaking her head, she smiled. "You make me complete."

In another situation he would have taken her in his arms and kissed her, but he had to settle for a smile and a telltale look.

Janet looked around and tried to absorb her surroundings. "This might have been his bench."

Sam looked behind them, but there were no bushes or anything near them where someone might hide or be hidden.

Picking up on something, Janet told them what she could sense. "A man who slept on this bench got up to relieve himself. He wouldn't go far from his possessions, so I'm guessing he went into the bushes behind us. When he came back, he found another man trying to steal his blanket. They argued, then the other man walked away cold and mad."

When nothing else came to mind, she was discouraged. "Maybe it wasn't the same man; this bench could have belonged to many homeless men since then."

"Maybe, maybe not. Let's go with that theory. What would a homeless do when his private space or possessions were threatened?" Sam asked.

"He would check his things to see if anything was missing, and either stick it out on the bench or leave to find somewhere else to stay. He may have come back to the same spot later or found a new one close by for a while." It was all speculation.

"He probably wouldn't go too far away, right? Maybe go find something to eat or drink and come back."

Janet nodded. They looked around trying to put themselves in this man's shoes for a different perspective.

"Look over there." Sam pointed in the direction of a power box behind some bushes. Two sections of privacy fence were meant to hide the power box. Part of the fence was broken. Tall bushes had been planted in front of it, but at the angle they were sitting, Sam could just see the box behind the fence.

Upon closer inspection of the metal box that covered the power connection for the lights in that area of the park was about three feet high, three feet wide, and four feet wide. Thick with frozen leaves and debris, the surrounding area could be hiding anything. Concentrating on the space between the box and the fence first, they started finding personal items—a stocking cap, a ragged scarf, a cup, a razor, and a toothbrush. Then Chris uncovered the fingers of a hand, black with decay. Digging out the body would take time, especially when they wanted to preserve as much evidence as possible.

Sam called dispatch to send the medical examiner, better tools and more equipment. Since he would be there most of the afternoon, Sam went back to where Janet waited not wanting her to sit in the cold for long. "Thanks for your help. I'll see you later."

"Sure. Call me later if you can't get away." She said.

"When this is all over, we are going to take some time off and go away together." Sam promised.

Janet knew there would always be another murder to solve, but she liked the idea of spending more time with Sam. She smiled. "That would be nice."

Sam nodded and might have said more, but another officer called to him. He smiled at her, and then walked away.

Janet walked back to the office at a brisk pace so she could get in where it was warm.

Chapter Twenty-Four

Michael's lawyer came to visit him everyday. The trial date was set for January. An analysis session was set up with the Psychiatrist hired by the Prosecution. Michael had agreed to cooperate. His lawyer kept telling him that the only way the insanity plea would work was if the two Psychiatrists were convinced he was indeed insane. Jonah had no doubt that his client was insane.

Dr. Adam Sinclair was the prosecution's appointed Psychiatrist for this trial. He interviewed Michael for two hours first asking questions on his childhood. Later he asked about his mother, her death, and delved into Michael's grudge against the homeless. Dr. Sinclair was good at his job and Michael told him how he would walk around following his victims before finally stabbing them to death. Michael told him how he chose his victims based upon how defenseless he thought they were. His mother was defenseless against her attacker.

Jonah was happy with the results of the first interview, but still thought it best if they had their own Psychiatrist to call to the stand. He set up the interview with Dr. Samuel Grey two days later.

Dr. Grey asked many of the same questions, but being curious about Michael's case, couldn't resist asking more personal questions. "Did you have a happy childhood? Who took care of you after your mother's death? Did you have lots of friends? How were your grades in school? Did you graduate from high school? Did you attend college?" These were questions that bothered Michael, mostly because he was in and out of foster homes and a product of the social service system the rest of the time. His childhood was not pleasant and he never developed any long lasting attachments to anyone during that time.

Finally, convinced that he had enough information for the trial, Dr. Grey asked one last question. "So what do you think about spending the rest of your life in an institution or a prison for the criminally insane?"

Michael stopped and looked at him, the anger building behind his eyes. "What?" Getting up he paced the room. "We're done. Send my lawyer in."

Jonah came into the interrogation room unaware of Michael's anger. He hadn't been watching the interview with the Psychiatrist knowing the interview was being taped. Thinking everything was going ahead fine as planned, there didn't seem to be any reason to worry about the interview's outcome. "So, how did it go?" Putting his briefcase on the table he started taking out the file with his notes, paper, and pen.

Michael leered at him from across the room, which Jonah had yet to notice. "I thought the whole purpose for this insanity plea was so I could go free. I thought they would put me in a hospital for treatment, and then I would be set free once they thought I was better. You lied to me." Michael almost choked on the words, he was so angry.

Jonah looked up. Fear quickly replaced surprise when he saw Michael's face. "I never promised you would be set free. I thought you understood this was a way to get out of the death penalty, a way to save your own life."

Michael walked quickly towards Jonah yelling. "You lied. You tricked me. I knew I couldn't trust anyone, but you tricked me." Picking up Jonah's pen from the table he jammed it into the shocked man's heart. Fear stood frozen upon his face as he slowly fell, knocking over the chair behind him.

Walking to the far end of the room, Michael paced back and forth. Police officers ran into the room, their first priority to put Michael in restraints and get him back to his cell. One officer knelt down by Jonah to check for a pulse, but found none. The pen appeared to have been driven through his heart.

Sam heard about the incident and came running. The coroner arrived. While watching Jonah's body was being put in a body bag, Sam called the District Attorney's office. They were hoping to get Michael arraigned that same day on the new charge so they could transfer him to a maximum security prison where he could be isolated from the other prisoners.

A new lawyer was appointed. The judge found it difficult to find someone who would take the case. He could have forced someone to do it, but based upon Michael's latest murder he thought that would be unfair.

Finally a seasoned lawyer, an ex-judge named Rooney Hara said he would take the case. He saw Michael for the first time standing outside his cell. When Michael would not talk to him, Rooney finally said. "I guess that means you want me to enter a plea of guilty?"

Michael looked at the lawyer and then went to his bunk to lie down. There was little doubt in anyone's mind, including Michael's, that he would get the death penalty.

Chapter Twenty-Five

With his chief's blessing, Sam took two weeks off. He had inherited Red's cabin after his death. At that time he was too busy with the case to make any decisions on what to do with it.

Now he had decided to spend his time off there. Sam had no idea what condition it was in or what it looked like. He planned on fixing it up either to use or to sell depending on how he felt about it after two weeks.

Red's cabin was on a small lake, which was now frozen over. As he pulled into the driveway, Sam was surprised. The cabin was indeed made of logs, but it was larger than the house Sam grew up in. As he went in the door, he saw a huge living room with a fireplace, a dining room, and a large eat in kitchen.

On the second floor, Sam found three bedrooms, all facing the lake with access to a large balcony. The master bedroom had its own bath, and the other two shared a bathroom.

Walking out onto the balcony, Sam decided to call Janet

on his cell phone. "You won't believe this place. It's in great condition. In fact, it looks like no one has ever lived here. There is a fireplace, but also a furnace. I'll have to check the propane, but I think this place will be great all year."

"I'm out on the balcony on the second floor looking out on the lake. It is freezing out here, but so beautiful with the setting sun shining on the ice. I can see some fishing shanties out in the middle of the lake and some guy on a snowmobile racing to shore." Sam described the scene before him.

Janet smiled at the image he tried to paint for her. "I pick up the rental car tomorrow, a four-wheel drive SUV. Do you want me to shop for groceries on my way?"

"No." Sam replied. "I have to go out and pick up some things anyway later. I'll get us enough to last a week. You sure you can't take more time off?"

Janet laughed. "We'll see. This is the first time I've ever been away from the office for longer than a day or two."

He knew she was still cautious about any commitment. Just spending the week together was a big step for her. Sam hoped that this vacation would take them to the next level of their relationship. "See you in the morning."

"This will be so great! I've never had a real vacation before." Janet was excited about getting away from the city and spending some real time with Sam.

He laughed. "I'll teach you how to relax and do absolutely nothing."

"Nothing?" She asked innocently.

"Well...? You'll just have to trust me on this."   Sam teased.

About the Author

When she was a little girl, Vicki told her mother that someday she would write a book. She has been writing since she made that promise. Now that dream has become a reality and writing has become a major part of her life. "Seeing the stories come to life on paper is exciting. All my stress is forgotten when I'm writing." In addition to writing, Vicki works in marketing and teaches college part-time. She lives in Northern Michigan with her husband, Matt, and their Airedale, Rosie. The Longs like to travel. A trip to New York City inspired the story in this book. This is Vicki Long's second book. Her first book, The Destiny Family, is available through 1stbooks at www.destinyfamily.com.

Printed in the United States
19041LVS00001B/33

MISSAUKEE DISTRICT LIBRARY